The
DEMON SWORD MASTER
of **Excalibur Academy**

The
DEMON SWORD MASTER
of **Excalibur Academy**

Yu Shimizu

ILLUSTRATION

Asagi Tosaka

The DEMON SWORD MASTER of Excalibur Academy

[3]

Yu Shimizu

ILLUSTRATION

Asagi Tosaka

YEN ON

NEW YORK

The Demon Sword Master of Excalibur Academy

Yu Shimizu

Translation by Roman Lempert
Cover art by Asagi Tosaka

SEIKEN GAKUIN NO MAKEN TSUKAI Vol. 3
©Yu Shimizu 2020
First published in Japan in 2020 by KADOKAWA CORPORATION, Tokyo.
English translation rights arranged with KADOKAWA CORPORATION, Tokyo
through TUTTLE-MORI AGENCY, INC., Tokyo.

English translation © 2021 by Yen Press, LLC

Yen On
150 West 30th Street, 19th Floor
New York, NY 10001

Visit us at yenpress.com
facebook.com/yenpress ★ twitter.com/yenpress
yenpress.tumblr.com ★ instagram.com/yenpress

First Yen On Edition: May 2021

Yen On is an imprint of Yen Press, LLC.
The Yen On name and logo are trademarks of Yen Press, LLC.

The publisher is not responsible for websites (or their content) that are not owned by the publisher.

Library of Congress Cataloging-in-Publication Data
Names: Shimizu, Yu, author. | Tosaka, Asagi, illustrator. | Lempert, Roman, translator.
Title: The demon sword master of Excalibur Academy / Yu Shimizu ; illustration by Asagi Tosaka ; translation by
Roman Lempert.
Other titles: Seiken gakuin no maken tsukai. English
Description: First Yen On edition. | New York : Yen On, 2020.
Identifiers: LCCN 2020017005 | ISBN 9781975308667 (v. 1 ; trade paperback) |
ISBN 9781975319151 (v. 2 ; trade paperback) | ISBN 9781975320706 (v. 3 ; trade paperback)
Subjects: CYAC: Fantasy. | Demonology—Fiction. | Reincarnation—Fiction.
Classification: LCC PZ7.1.S5174 De 2020 | DDC [Fic]—dc23
LC record available at https://lccn.loc.gov/2020017005

ISBNs: 978-1-9753-2070-6 (paperback)
978-1-9753-2071-3 (ebook)

1 3 5 7 9 10 8 6 4 2

LSC-C

Printed in the United States of America

A shrill siren echoed through the darkened shelter. Riselia and Regina, both only nine years old, sat huddled together, their shoulders shivering in fear. Eight hours had passed since the Stampede began. Through the constant blaring of alarms, the two girls could hear the distant sounds of distorted howls. A swarm of Voids was closing in on the Third Assault Garden's center.

If those monstrous things found Riselia and Regina, it would be the end of the girls. Those terrifying creatures would easily shred their way through this shelter's shutters. Riselia's father, Duke Edward Ray Crystalia, had half forced his young daughter into the safe room and bid her his final farewell.

"Father, I'll fight the Voids, too!" Riselia had insisted.

"No. You still haven't awakened to the power of a Holy Sword," Duke Crystalia scolded his daughter, who had clung to him just as he was about to depart.

"...A Holy Sword... But...!"

Riselia's father squatted down, gently patting her fair, silvery locks.

"Don't worry. The Dark Lord will surely appear in this world someday."

"The Dark Lord... Isn't that a bad person?"

The Dark Lord was a character who appeared in the fairy tales Riselia's father would always tell her. He was supposed to be a king who ruled over evil monsters.

After seeing his confused daughter cock her head, Duke Crystalia cracked a bitter smile. "That's right. A bad Dark Lord will appear in this dying world someday, to—"

"...?"

Duke Crystalia wasn't so much explaining it to his daughter as he was speaking to himself. Even years later, Riselia struggled to discern what her father had thought when he'd said those words. There'd been an undeniable earnestness to his tone, a keen emotion that hadn't felt like he was merely trying to cheer his daughter up.

A bad Dark Lord will come to this world to...

The cries of the Voids grew nearer, and the lights in the shelter went out. Riselia and Regina sat terrified in total darkness. Riselia prayed, as hard as she could, that the Dark Lord her father spoke of would appear.

Then...

In year 58 of the Integrated Human Calendar, the Third Assault Garden, Crystalia, was destroyed in the midst of a Void Stampede.

CHAPTER 1

THE MASKED DARK LORD

That dream again...

Riselia Crystalia awoke from her restless slumber and wiped the cold sweat from her brow with her sleeping gown sleeve. Even six years after the Voids had destroyed the Third Assault Garden, Riselia was still plagued by that terrible nightmare.

Even with my body like this, I guess I still dream..., Riselia mused as she shook her head to banish the lingering unpleasantness from her mind. She sat up and opened the curtains of her window.

The morning sunlight shined upon the locks of Riselia's argent hair. Stretching slightly, the young woman groggily rubbed her ice-blue eyes. Looking out the window, she spied a flock of birds perching on a tree in the courtyard.

Unfortunately, they weren't cute little feathered friends, whose chirping signaled the coming of a refreshing morning, but rather...

"Caw! Caw! Caw!"

A murder of large, scary-faced crows had filled the trees beyond Riselia's window. Their eerie shrieks almost seemed to announce that Riselia had risen from bed.

...There's more of them now..., Riselia noted to herself, her

expression contorting into a stiff frown. Crows had started flocking around her often as of late.

...Do I really smell like a corpse?

Riselia sniffed at her clothes, but the only scent she caught was the floral aroma of her soap. According to Leonis, creatures of the night like crows and bats tended to gather around vampires, as they were the supreme beings of darkness.

"The fact that they like me is nice, but..." Riselia sighed, looking out the window. *If any more of them show up, people are gonna start spreading weird rumors about the dorm...*

The Hræsvelgr dormitory rested on the outskirts of Excalibur Academy's vast grounds. Because it looked older than its surrounding structures, people already treated it as a spooky mansion of sorts. Lately, there'd been rumors about a shadow in the shape of a girl and a large black dog wandering around the place after dark. The gossip really sounded like ghost stories. If crows started gathering around the dorm, people truly would start thinking the place was a haunted house.

Not that they'd be technically wrong. A vampire *did* live in the Hræsvelgr dorm, after all.

Brushing her fingers through her slightly disheveled hair, Riselia rose from her bed. She and Leonis planned to hold a training match this morning, so she had decided to wake up a bit earlier than usual.

"Leo, time to get up!" Riselia called after getting to her feet. However, when she opened the door and made to enter the adjacent chamber...

"...?!"

Her hand froze on the doorknob. Standing inside the room was a girl in a maid's outfit holding a mop and bucket. She was cleaning the floor. She had sleek black hair cut to shoulder length and crimson eyes the color of twilight. Her gaze met Riselia's straight on.

"..."

"..."

Both young women stood frozen for a few seconds. Then, the maid girl's face screwed up in an expression that seemed to say, "Oh, drat."

"...Huh...? Wh-who are you...?" Riselia blinked a few times and rubbed her eyes. Surprisingly, when she took another look, the maid girl was gone.

◆

"Shit, they're gonna corner us at this rate!"

"...We have to go on the offensive here. It's not like we can hide forever."

"That's reckless. We don't stand a chance against Holy Swords men with the weapons we have..."

Several sets of footsteps echoed through a dark corridor, as did voices that sounded similar to bestial growls. Golden eyes shone through the darkness. This was the Seventh Assault Garden's seventh sector—the special demi-human protection ward.

The underground passageways that ran beneath the artificial biotope's forest were occupied by armed beastmen. They were remnants of the Sovereign Wolves, a terrorist organization that opposed the Integrated Empire.

Two weeks ago, their comrades had tried to seajack the royal warship *Hyperion* in order to abduct Altiria Ray O'ltriese, the fourth princess. The Excalibur Academy students on board had opposed the Sovereign Wolves, however, and the operation had failed. The radical group's leader, Bastea Colossuf, died with several other leading members, leaving the organization on the brink of collapse.

And now, they were being pursued by a group of the empire's Holy Swordsmen.

"If only we were compatible with the Demon Swords, too..." The beastman leading what remained of the Sovereign Wolves growled in frustration.

"...Dammit, they're coming!"

Several figures appeared ahead of the fleeing extremists, blocking the underground passage. Their white uniforms stood out in the dark. It was an elite force of Holy Swordsmen.

"Remnants of the Sovereign Wolves! You are under arrest for the crime of high treason!"

The Holy Swordsmen totaled four. The beastmen greatly outnumbered them. However, the power of Holy Swords, a boon granted only to humans, proved enough to overturn that advantage.

""""Holy Sword, Activate!"""" the Holy Swordsmen intoned in unison, their voices reverberating through the underground corridor.

"Dammit!" One beastman howled as he and his fellows charged the Holy Swordsmen in desperation.

It was reckless. While the demi-humans' physical prowess exceeded the humans', they had no way of overcoming four Holy Swords.

I know that, dammit! the leader of the beastmen thought to himself bitterly.

That was when...

"Demonic Eyes, Curse These Fearless Ones—Vraid!" a new voice boomed from somewhere unseen.

Not a moment later, there was an explosion of light, and the Holy Swordsmen froze in place, their weapons still drawn. They now looked for all the world like silent statues.

"Wh-what just...?" The beastmen were speechless.

"—I've been looking for you... Finding you cost me valuable time."

"...?!"

From the depths of the underground passage, a pale-blue light drifted in the musky darkness. Behind that glow, the faint sound of footsteps clicking against the floor reverberated through the close confines of the tunnel.

A dark, humanoid figure clad in a pitch-black overcoat appeared. There stood what looked like darkness given human form. Its face was covered by a silvery mask shaped like a skull.

"Wh-who the hell are you...?!"

The beastmen held up their weapons, their bodies trembling. However...

"Fools."

The shade slightly raised its right hand. That simple motion was all that was needed to twist the weapons in the demi-humans' hands as easily as dough. The useless things fell to the ground.

"What?!"

"Kneel. You are in my presence," the shadow demanded, its voice bearing down like physical pressure and forcing the beast-men's knees to buckle.

The ominous presence overflowing from this figure made their robust bodies shiver like leaves. The beastmen were the very symbol of the natural world's law of survival of the fittest; their reactions were instinctual.

The shade before them was a monster of a far higher order than they—an absolute sovereign, made to reign over this world.

"You would raise your weapons against me...?" The shadow took another step closer. "Count yourselves fortunate, for I am magnanimous. Had Gazoth, the Lord of Beasts been in my position, you would already be dead."

"Aah, aaaah... Aaaaaaaaaaaah...!"

None of the beastmen could raise their heads in the face of the dark specter's overwhelming pressure. The insurgents fell prostrate, and the shadow tossed a small sack in front of them.

"Wh-what is this?" the lion-headed leader of the remnants asked.

"Your leader. His name was Bastea, I believe? These are his ashes."

"What?!"

"When I found him on that ship, he had already been reduced to dust. Even in such a state, my Realm of Death sorcery could have resurrected him as an undead monster, but, well, I had no duty to do so."

"Who are you...? No. Who might you be, mighty one?"

"I am a Dark Lord."

"A Dark Lord...?"

"The Undead King, he who reigns over death and all connected to it. The true, legitimate ruler of this world." As the shade's voice echoed, the sinister aura that spilled from it grew more intense. Suffocated by the fierce, encroaching presence of death, a few of the beastmen fell unconscious.

"U-ugh... Oooh, aaah...!"

"Fear not. I stand before you to repay a favor."

"A—A favor...?"

"Not to you, but to your distant ancestors. The Shamar clan, the Zaith clan, the Zakar clan. The beastmen warriors once served bravely as vanguards for the Dark Lords' Armies."

Those few Sovereign Wolves who were still conscious answered the shadow's words with confusion. Ancestors? What was this monster saying?

"You who oppose the empire..." The so-called Dark Lord offered his hand. "Become my subordinates and serve in the Dark Lords' Armies." The shade's clear voice echoed through the underground tunnel.

"Y-you want us...the remnants of the Sovereign Wolves, to serve under you, great one?"

"Correct. You shall be my minions, acting in my name to achieve my lofty goals. I shan't force you, however. You may choose your fates freely. However..." The Dark Lord pointed at the statues behind them. "You haven't long to decide. Within several minutes, the petrification on those people will end."

"...!"

The eye sockets of the shadow's skeletal mask blazed with an eerie light. A wrong answer here could leave the beastmen petrified, just like these Holy Swordsmen. The beastmen exchanged glances. Either way, their alternative was to be caught by the empire and sent to the gallows. They didn't know what this inexplicable monster was after, but...

"U-understood." The lion-headed beastmen stood and bowed low before the Dark Lord. "The remnants of the Sovereign Wolves will serve you, great one."

It felt as if the skull mask sneered evilly at them.

"Very well. From now on, you shall call yourselves the Dark Lord's Shadows."

"Y-yes. By your will." The beastmen terrorists fell to their knees.

"Then I shall give you your first order—" But as the Dark Lord swung up his hand, an untimely beeping sound filled the underground passage. "H-huh, wh-what...?!" The shadowy figure recoiled in surprise.

"—eo. Leo! Where are you right now?!"

The voice died down with another beep.

"…"

An awkward air hung over the place. The terrorists looked at each other.

"Heh-heh… Ah-ha-ha-ha-ha-ha!" The Dark Lord suddenly started laughing, flapping his dark overcoat. "Obey My Will, Land, and Become an Eternal Maze! Create Labyrinth!"

As the specter chanted some kind of spell, the ground rumbled and lit up, forming a staircase leading farther down.

"Wh-what is this…?"

"I created an underground complex here. Make it your base and operate from there for the time being," the shadow instructed over its shoulder after turning away. It then disappeared, leaving the stupefied beastmen behind. The terrorists could only gawk at the entrance to the labyrinth, their mouths hanging open in amazement.

◆

Back in a dormitory room, a shadow bubbled up near his bed. From within rose a dark silhouette, clad in an ebon overcoat.

"Mantle of Illusions, Detach," a muffled voice commanded.

The darkness enveloping the shade's body came undone, and it was sucked into the shadows. A pair of small feet touched down on the floor.

"…My word. Keeping up that act does leave me feeling quite stiff."

A ten-year-old boy sporting a school uniform had stepped out from that tall shadow. Standing in front of a full-length mirror, the child heaved a deep sigh. His face had handsome—if young and childish—features. His black hair was slightly unkempt and continually disobedient, and he wasn't tall enough to eclipse even half the mirror.

When I look like this, I can't conjure up even a lick of dignity and awe. This unassuming appearance did lull his enemies into carelessness, though, and it was ideal for fitting into a crowd. *Regardless, I did manage to create a foothold toward the reformation of the Dark Lords' Armies.*

This boy, the Dark Lord Leonis Death Magnus, smirked in satisfaction. The Sovereign Wolves were an anti-imperial armed terrorist organization made up of demi-humans. A few days ago, they had lost their leader in a seajacking incident, leaving Leonis free to claim the group's remnants for his own.

Their ranks included far more than just the physically capable beastmen. The Sovereign Wolves were made up of elves and lizardmen, too. Both were unique species possessing valuable traits. Leonis was confident they could be of use.

That said, they didn't seem to have any direct involvement with the dark elf woman who had produced the Demon Swords, but Leonis decided he'd look into that matter separately.

Still... Leonis took a terminal out of his pocket and eyed it reproachfully. *My minion is a bit too overprotective.*

Sighing bitterly, he opened the door to the living room...

"Aaah! L-Leo?!"

...Only to find a girl standing there, clad in just her underwear. Shining silvery hair and skin as white as the virgin snow. Her hair was a bit damp, as she'd likely just got out of the shower. The young woman stood frozen, her hands still on the hook of her bra. Her face was steadily reddening by the second.

"Ah... I-I'm sorry!"

Leonis hurriedly squeezed his eyes shut and turned away, but the image of the girl's plump breasts and lithe limbs had already been burned into his mind. The sound of shifting fabric filled his ears for some time, until eventually...

"...You can turn around now, Leo."

Leonis did just that, fixing his gaze on the now fully clothed Riselia.

"I'm sorry, I must have surprised you," Riselia apologized as she tied a hair ribbon. Her blue uniform complemented her pale skin tone perfectly.

"N-no, I should be the one apologizing..."

"Where were you, by the way? You weren't in your room. I was looking for you."

"Erm... I was out for some morning exercise..."

"Exercise?" Riselia pouted adorably. "I'd have come along if you'd said something."

"I mean, we already have our daily training curriculum. So you shouldn't overdo it!" Leonis shook his head.

Riselia's recent growth was astounding. Not only did she possess fantastic intuition, but also a drive to improve. Training her was satisfying. However, she was also hardworking to the point of overexertion. Pushing one's limits could lead to collapse.

In that regard, Leonis wished Riselia would be a bit more careful with herself. Even an undead vampire would grow exhausted if she was to deplete her mana.

"Are you all right, Lady Selia? I heard a scream," Regina's voice called from the corridor.

"Ah, yes, I'm fine. It was just Leo," Riselia replied hurriedly.

◆

"—I put a lot of effort into breakfast today," Regina proudly proclaimed. She was wearing her usual maid uniform, and her hands rested confidently on her waist. "Eat up."

Regina's golden hair was tied up in pigtails, and her large, lively eyes were a shade of green. If Riselia could be likened to the kind, gentle moon, Regina had the atmosphere of the bright sun.

"It looks great," Riselia commented.

"Hee-hee. Today I made your favorite, Lady Selia! Fluffy pancakes."

Sitting on the table was a batch of pancakes with lots of honey, a salad of fruit and vegetables, sunny-side-up eggs, yogurt, and coffee. Riselia usually handled breakfast, but two times a week, Regina came over to prepare it. According to Regina herself, making meals for Riselia kept her maid skills honed.

"After all, if I leave you to handle the food yourself, you'll just end up eating military rations, Lady Selia."

"I-I've been making breakfast every day recently!" Riselia shot back, her cheeks a bit rosy. "I mean, I've got Leo to look after, too."

Riselia was a decent cook in her own right, but she was no match for a full-fledged maid like Regina.

"Want me to spoon-feed you, kid?" Regina asked Leonis with a smirk.

"I—I can eat just fine on my own, thank you!" Leonis snapped back, his heart skipping a beat. He carried a bite-size piece of a pancake to his lips. "...It really is good," he praised with pleasant surprise as he chewed and swallowed the piece.

The texture was nice and soft, and the sweet taste of honey filled his mouth. Its surface was crunchy. It had been expertly prepared. Leonis always thought the human body and its dependence on food were a nuisance, but...

...*This isn't that bad*, the Dark Lord thought to himself, satisfied.

"Heh-heh. You're so cute, kid. Makes it all worth it."

"Leo, you need to eat some lettuce, too. We got it from the vegetable garden," Riselia chided, shoveling some raw greens onto his plate. She seemed rather insistent.

She isn't doing it to make my blood smoother, is she...? Leonis had been suspecting as much for a while now.

"What's wrong, Leo?"

"Nothing," Leonis replied evasively, bringing a mug of coffee to his lips.

...Coffee really is good in the mornings.

This beverage hadn't existed a thousand years ago, but Leonis was growing fond of it. Its ebon color was like darkness made liquid. A fitting drink for a Dark Lord if there ever was one. Of course, it was too bitter straight, so Leonis added plenty of sugar to it.

"Is it just me, or have there been a lot of crows around our dorm recently?" Regina remarked, glancing out the window.

"R-really?" Riselia stuttered, a bit flustered. "Maybe it's your imagination."

"Should I drive them away?" Regina suggested, pantomiming the action of taking a shot with a gun.

"What? No! The poor things."

"You're too kind, Lady Selia. That's what I like about you, though," Regina appended with a wry smile and a shrug. "Still, people already call this dorm a haunted mansion. The birds aren't going to help."

"Really?" Leonis pressed.

"Yeah, there are rumors about some girl's ghost and a large black dog walking around..."

"Oh, that's right! I actually saw the ghost girl this morning!" Riselia raised her voice after suddenly recalling the incident from earlier.

"You did?" Regina asked.

"Yeah. She was really cute, and she was dressed like a maid—"

"So, me?" Regina pointed at herself.

"No, she had short black hair. And she was cleaning Leo's room."

"...!" Leonis almost gagged on his coffee. "M-maybe your eyes were playing tricks on you!" he managed between coughs.

"...Yeah, maybe. She was gone the moment I blinked."

"Sounds like you were still sleepy. Speaking of, I heard today we have a joint training session and a practice match?" Leonis was doing his best to pivot the topic of conversation to something else.

"Oh, right, this is your first time seeing a sparring session between different platoons."

Practice matches were a central part of Excalibur Academy's training program. They were usually held earlier in the year, but the Stampede in the Seventh Assault Garden several weeks ago had pushed back the school's schedule.

"Our opponents this time are the eleventh platoon, from Fafnir dorm," Regina told Leonis, showing him her terminal. "They're a higher-ranked squad led by Fenris Edelritz."

There was a picture of a girl projected on the device's monitor. She looked like an affluent young lady. What's more, Leonis recognized her. She was a student from the executive committee who had introduced herself to him during the party aboard the *Hyperion*.

"Erm, is there any point to having Holy Swordsmen fight each other?" The tactless question slipped from Leonis's lips the second it crossed his mind.

Holy Swords were supposedly a power granted to the human race to fight the twisted creatures known as Voids.

"It's said that Holy Swords competing against each other encourages their growth," Riselia explained, holding up her index finger.

"Growth?"

"Yes. By clashing against each other, Holy Swords can change their forms."

"My Drag Howl only had its cannon mode at first. It couldn't shift into a pistol until later down the line," Regina added.

"I see. So they do it to help the weapons mature...," Leonis whispered to himself.

Holy Swords were a power granted by the planet, the tools that allowed humanity to strike back at the Voids. Their might was a fundamentally different sort than sorcery, which was based on the laws of nature. A thousand years ago, humans' comparatively low mana capacities and weak physical capabilities had made them inferior to the elves and demi-humans. But in the end, it was humanity that survived the past millennia. They had endured and achieved a technological standard high enough to build these advanced Assault Gardens.

The evolution of Holy Swords. It's as if the weapons are a manifestation of humankind's strength as a species, Leonis mused to himself.

"It's also my first training match since I got my Holy Sword, so we have to give it our all!" Riselia proclaimed, pumping her fists. "If you get good grades during the training match, you get invited to the Holy Sword Blade Dance Festival at the capital."

"Really?" Leonis asked, curious to hear more.

"Yeah. It's held once a year, and Holy Swordsmen are selected from every Assault Garden to participate in a celebration of swordsmanship. It's pretty much out of reach for us, but..." Riselia trailed off.

"You never know," Regina said. "You have a Holy Sword now, and we have the kid on our side, too."

"You're right." Riselia nodded. "For now, let's put our all into winning the sparring match today."

...Hmm. The capital, eh? Not bad.

The capital. The first Assault Garden to be built and the central hub of the Integrated Empire. When the Dark Lords' Armies rose again, Leonis planned to seize control of that city.

If we get selected to participate in this Holy Sword Blade Dance

Festival, I could scout out the capital without drawing attention to myself.
Quite unlike Riselia's pure excitement, it was malicious intent that
brewed in Leonis's heart.

◆

Dark-green light illuminated the half-circle-shaped space. At the
center of the chamber, something undulated gently. The glow was
coming from a mana furnace, a large, crystal-like apparatus capable of powering a massive Assault Garden.

The device gathered the mana flowing through underground
ley lines and converted it into an enormous amount of energy—a
crystallization of human wisdom. And sitting atop that container
holding the mana furnace in place was something humanoid...

A beautiful girl. Her pale frame was completely exposed, and
her long hair pulsed with light in time to the mana furnace's flick-
ering. Half her body was fused into the furnace, and countless
cables were connected to her spinal cord, sharing the mana the
immense machine supplied to the city.

The young woman's eyes lacked the light of intelligence. Her
hollow gaze simply stared into the dark.

"Yes, I see things are coming along nicely. Splendid." An
ill-fitting, cheerful voice resounded through the chamber.

A man appeared, the sound of his footsteps clicking against
the floor. He was young and dressed in white, priestly attire. His
hair was alabaster, and his blue eyes had a gentle glint to them.
His mere presence made the place feel like some grand cathedral.

The young man looked up at the woman fused into the mana
furnace and smiled.

"For now, it seems it's a success. Well, we did offer up several
hundred Demon Swords as a sacrifice. If it didn't work, I'd be quite

livid with those old cultists." He placed a hand on the shining mana furnace, the smirk still on his lips. "Soon, it will be time for you to awaken—our prophesized goddess."

◆

Void habitats were at all times filled with a dense miasma. They were dark, polluted areas unsuitable for humans. It was from one such gloomy, repugnant place that *it* appeared. Sailing along the ocean's surface was a titanic man-made structure—one of the final fortifications built to safeguard humanity from the apostles of emptiness.

It was a ruined city said to have been destroyed in the Stampede six years ago.

CHAPTER 2

TRAINING MATCH

"—The enemy is holed up in their base deep in the forest field. Be careful."

"Roger that. We're moving in, but we'll stay alert." Riselia turned around, answering Elfiné's call through her communication terminal. "Let's go, Leo."

"Right."

The two of them advanced through the woods. The combat field selected for this training match was a replica of a boreal forest. And if need be, it could be changed to adjust to any terrain or environment. What struck Leonis as most surprising was that this change of terrain could be done in a mere sixteen hours.

...Human technology truly has come a long way.

Leonis marveled, taking in the artificial, yet realistic, woodland surroundings. Sunlight coursed down through the greenery. In terms of sheer size, the area was no larger than Necrozoa's arena. Leonis had often had ogres, trolls, and other such monsters pitted against one another there.

However, if Leonis had wanted naval battles in those days, water channeled from nearby lakes and rivers would have been required. Similarly, desert battlegrounds meant large loads of sand needed to be hauled in. In that regard, this facility was far more sophisticated and well-equipped.

While Leonis thought on such things, Riselia suddenly stopped in her tracks in the middle of a small forest clearing. Her gaze was fixed forward.

"I think there's a trap ahead."

Thanks to preliminary research, Leonis and Riselia already knew that one of the enemy team's Holy Sword wielders had the power to produce snares and other gimmicks. And this spot, with its good visibility, was a perfect place to set a trap.

"Elfiné, could you check if there are enemies ahe—?"

"There's a sniper by the flag."

"..." Riselia considered that for a moment.

Leonis kept his lips sealed, not offering her any aid. Riselia understood why, though. It was more than Leonis merely gauging her abilities. Everything that went on in this match was broadcast, so he didn't want to expose too much of his powers.

...How will you overcome this?

The rules of the bout were simple enough. Defeating an opposing team member earned you points based on that student's grade. Additionally, each team had a base set up somewhere in the field, and capturing the enemy team's flag from that base also earned points. Every match had a score threshold, and the first group to meet or exceed it won.

Sakuya was currently assaulting the rival squad's base. She held the record for single-handedly slaying Voids, which meant the opponent was likely to be most wary of her. The opposing team had gathered their defenses to meet Sakuya's attack. Fenris was leading them.

By contrast, Riselia had only recently gained her Holy Sword, and Leonis looked like a ten-year-old boy. They weren't seen as a significant threat. Seizing upon that, the two of them snuck around, intending to flank the enemy.

There weren't many points they could strike at on their own, but Riselia was aiming to take down one of the opposing team's less defended bases.

Either way, speed is of the essence here.

Elfiné and Regina had stayed behind to protect their own flag. Elfiné's Holy Sword was significantly weaker than it had once been, and she now specialized in scouting and information gathering. Thus, the only effective defending member was Regina. Leaving the task of safeguarding the base solely to her was a bold decision. While Regina was undoubtedly skilled, a sniper operating without a partner to guard them was asking to be rushed by the enemy.

"I could just blow away the forest with my Drag Howl, though." Regina had made a dangerous suggestion.

Despite such a foreboding statement, Regina's anti-Void annihilation cannon, the Drag Howl, actually had its power significantly inhibited during the match. All antipersonnel Holy Swords were required to limit their strength for sparring. In so many words, it was like landing blows with the dull side of a blade.

However, Holy Swords took all shapes. Those that couldn't restrain their power adequately were forbidden from participating in these bouts.

We have to swoop in and take down the enemy base at once while Sakuya has their attention.

Leonis and Riselia's options were to either go around this clearing or push straight ahead. And they didn't have much time to mull over their choice.

"—Let's go around. This way," Riselia decided, taking off into the nearby bushes with her Bloody Sword in hand.

That's why you're worthy of being my right-hand woman, Leonis applauded silently.

A Dark Lord's general would have charged forward knowingly, intent on crushing any cunning traps with sheer strength. Such was the established, ruthless practice, and doing so showed off the Dark Lord's power and cut away at the opponent's morale. A Dark Lord should scoff at the idea of petty tricks.

However...

That way of thinking led to the Dark Lords' Armies' downfall.

Leonis preferred to charge his enemies headfirst and crush them underfoot, too. And this was why he appreciated the fact that his right-hand woman was cautious enough to avoid a trap.

Riselia's choice was praiseworthy to Leonis. Still, had she chosen to charge into the trap, he likely would have complimented her for showing the pluck expected of a Dark Lord's servant. It was relatively easy to surmise that Leonis had a soft spot for his favored minion.

◆

"Mm. They're doing pretty well," Instructor Diglassê said of the eighteenth platoon from a seat in the academy sports grounds.

When Leonis had first entered the academy, she'd overseen his duel with an upperclassman, Muselle. The current bout was being projected onto a large monitor on the academy's premises. Students and civilians alike were allowed access to the school grounds to spectate.

That said, there weren't many spectators right now. Part of the reason was that this was a morning match. The more outstanding issue was that the eighteenth platoon didn't inspire much interest. Plus, they were up against the Fafnir dorm, one of the best at Excalibur Academy. Many had decided the outcome of the match before it had even started.

Apparently, some of the students were committing unofficial gambling, but they decided this wasn't a match worth gambling on. Sakuya was a skilled fencer, to be sure, but she didn't function well in team settings. Elfiné's Holy Sword had lost its original power, and Regina's strongpoint—her large cannon—was unusable in this match. This left the leader, Riselia, who'd only recently awakened to her Holy Sword. She'd beaten Muselle in battle recently, but many believed she'd won by way of the element of surprise, since it was her Holy Sword's first showing.

And lastly, there was the eighteenth platoon's newest addition— the ten-year-old boy. He was seen as baggage that would only weigh down his team.

How will this turn out, I wonder...?

♦

Two shadows raced through the thicket, heedless of the poor footing. Riselia charged her feet with mana and kicked from tree to tree as she sped like the wind.

"Leo, can you keep up?"

"—Yes, I'm fine," the Dark Lord answered, soaring right behind her.

Who do you take me for, woman?

Leonis had used a Shadow Striding spell, allowing him to move with Riselia's shadow. So long as this magic was in effect, he was merged with the shadows and was capable of phasing through the trees. Shary had taught Leonis this spell, and it had proved quite useful over the years.

Suddenly, Leonis heard a something whistle through the air. A sharp bolt of light skimmed past Riselia's cheek and disappeared into the bushes behind them.

"An archer...," Riselia whispered.

Bows were a standard sort of ranged Holy Sword. Had Riselia picked a route with less cover, the archer would have shot her down. Thankfully, this roundabout path, full of curves and trees, had proven troublesome for the enemy. They hadn't been able to get a clean shot.

"Did you expect the sniper to aim for us?" asked Leonis.

"No, it was just intuition. I got the feeling taking that route would be dangerous."

Intuition, hmm? Wonderful, Leonis thought.

Thwp, thwp, thwp!

Three more bolts whizzed through the air. Riselia kicked off the ground, her ice-blue eyes shining crimson with mana. She sprinted through the dense trees and drew her blade, accurately spotting another speeding projectile and cutting it down mid-flight.

"I see you're getting used to using your vampiric eyesight," Leonis remarked.

"It's thanks to your training," Riselia replied.

The young woman's improvements weren't only limited to a growing mastery of her undead physical abilities. Practice against Leonis's skeletons had greatly improved her swordsmanship as well.

Seeing this minion of mine grow is fascinating.

Perhaps getting desperate, the archer unleashed another flurry of bolts, which rained down on Leonis and Riselia. However...

"Dimud!" Leonis fired a simple Devil Whirlwind spell to deflect the projectiles.

"Aaaaaaaaaaaaaah!" Riselia charged forward, cutting down the trees in her way.

Beyond the close-knit foliage, she and Leonis found an open spot at the foot of a hill. Looking up toward the peak of the mound, they spied a girl holding a crossbow-type Holy Sword. She was stationed right beside a point flag.

"...How did she get here this fast?!" The surprise was plain on the sniper's face. She hurriedly made to loose another bolt, but...

"Got you!"

Riselia unleashed the mana gathered in her legs and jumped up into the air. She landed lightly atop the hill and closed in on the crossbow girl. In a melee battle, Riselia had a clear advantage.

Unfortunately...

"*Grrrrrrrrrrrrrr!*"

Two wolves made of ice appeared from behind the rocks and rushed Riselia.

"...Miss Selia?!" Leonis called out, flying up the cliff a moment after her.

Riselia reflexively held up a hand to guard her vitals. One of the Frost Wolves sank its fangs into her arm, which froze solid on the spot.

"Heh. I knew you would come here, Riselia Crystalia! And her valet boy, too!"

Standing atop the rocks was a blue-eyed girl with platinum-blond hair—the eleventh platoon's captain, Fenris Edelritz.

"...What are you doing here, Fenris?!" Riselia raised her voice in surprise as she leaped back to get some distance.

Fenris should have been busy with Sakuya, who was charging into the base from a forward position.

"Naturally, I came to settle the score with you," Fenris replied, twisting a strand of hair around her finger.

Five Frost Wolves formed to surround Riselia.

"No, I mean, what happened to Sakuya—?"

"Heh-heh. That girl is quite strong with a sword but weak to distractions. I believe some of my pets are playing around with her right about now."

...They lured her into the woods.

Fenris had snuck here while keeping Sakuya overwhelmed with

her Holy Sword's autonomous Frost Wolves. By staying beneath the cover of the forest canopy, where she'd been hard to detect, she'd used the wolves to slip past Elfiné's tracking.

"A forest is my preferred stage for battle." Fenris smiled confidently. "Two of my platoon's strongest attackers should be storming your base as we speak. Miss Elfiné and your maid will be no match for them. Victory is ours!"

"...!"

It was true that guarding the flag would be difficult for those two alone. However...

"Sakuya once told me that a battle can always be decided by claiming the commander's head," Riselia said, glaring up at Fenris.

"...What are you implying, exactly?"

"That I just need to defeat you before your team wins!" Riselia shouted, releasing the mana in her body. The ice around her left arm shattered with a clear, shrill sound.

◆

"Oh, is that the mishmash platoon?"

"Seriously? They've got a kid with them. They should know this isn't some game."

Students who passed by the spectator seats snickered as they watched the fight on the monitor. It was then that a girl sitting in the front row abruptly rose to her feet.

"...L-Leo is definitely gonna win!" she shouted at the sneering onlookers.

Hmm? Diglassê found herself smiling with curiosity.

The one who'd spoken up was an adorable seven-, maybe eight-year-old girl with black, shoulder-length hair. Judging by her attire, she was a refugee.

"...Huh? Who're you?" The students glared at the young girl with evident displeasure.

She did not back down, though.

"Tessera's right! Leo and Riselia saved our orphanage!" Another girl, this one with walnut-colored hair, stood in front of the black-haired one, as if to protect her.

"M-Millet...!" A bespectacled boy anxiously pulled at her arm.

"What, are you their friends or something?" A male student shrugged and turned his eyes back to the screen. "Well, I've got bad news for you. There's no way they'll win."

"Yep. Not against Fenris and the eleventh platoon," another boy agreed, waving his hand dismissively.

But then...

"I would say these children have a better eye for this than any of you do," a charming voice interjected.

"...?"

Everyone turned to see a girl in a maid's attire occupying one of the spectator seats and munching on a doughnut.

...*When did she get here?!* Diglassê was taken aback. She hadn't sensed the girl's approach at all.

◆

"—Hmph! A failure like you cannot hope to win against me!"

"*Grrrrrrrrrrrr!*"

At Fenris's order, the five Frost Wolves swooped down on Riselia.

"Hyaaah!" Riselia squatted down and brandished the Bloody Sword. She slashed through one of the frozen constructs and, spinning in place, bashed her weapon's pommel into another. In one fluid motion, she then reassumed a defensive stance.

"What?!" Fenris's eyes widened with shock at Riselia's swift, precise bladework.

...She's experienced with fighting groups of enemies after training against my skeleton beasts.

"I'm not a failure anymore!" Mana burst from Riselia's legs as she lunged forward.

"...I won't let you!" The crossbow girl, who had been lying hidden behind the rocks, fired a bolt of light at Riselia.

"How boorish," Leonis whispered, and he tapped his Staff of Sealed Sins against the ground. In the blink of an eye, shadows slithered up like serpents and swallowed the projectile.

"...Huh?!"

Hidden Snake was an elementary shadowmancer's spell. The shadowy serpents screeched as they swiftly coiled around the archer.

"N-noooo... Mmmg, nnng!"

The crossbow girl let out a shriek that was quickly reduced to muffled whimpers. The ebon snakes coiled around her, becoming a black cocoon. With the archer handily dispatched, Leonis turned his attention to Riselia.

She'd jumped up to the ledge and was bringing her Holy Sword down at Fenris.

"Aaaaaaaaaaah!"

Riselia swung with her blade's blunt side, meaning a direct blow would still knock Fenris unconscious. However...

"...You're still just as naive, Riselia!" Fenris cried, taking a backward step to evade the attack. Two Frost Wolves leaped to Fenris's side to guard her. Riselia took another step closer, but at that moment, Fenris thrust her hands forward and shouted, "Holy Sword, Mode Shift! Freezing Knuckles!"

The two Frost Wolves turned into swirling spirals of ice and air that enveloped Fenris's fists. Like Regina's Drag Howl, Fenris's Holy Sword was capable of changing into another weapon. Fenris's Frost Wolves growled as they settled over her clenched hands and blocked Riselia's slash.

"Oh no!" Riselia gasped.

Fenris caught the other girl's blade with one hand, and she threw a punch with the other.

...Despite how she looks, it seems she's a pugilist, Leonis observed.

"Kah... Nng...!"

Riselia's body went flying and then landed on the ground with a bounce before tumbling a few paces. Yet, her grip on her Holy Sword didn't slacken—proof of the young woman's pride.

Although Riselia had been knocked to the ground, Fenris refused to let up, dashing forward. "I'm not done yet!"

"...!" Riselia scrambled to her feet and tried to back away, but...

"...My leg...?!"

A Frost Wolf had bitten down on one of her legs, holding it in place.

"Ha, this match is finished!" Fenris exclaimed victoriously, closing in on Riselia while brandishing her Freezing Knuckles.

...I suppose a bit of help wouldn't hurt.

Leonis, ever the softy when it came to his minion, began chanting a shadow magic spell. Before he completed it, however...

"...lose..."

Riselia's ice-blue eyes flickered with crimson. A whirlwind of mana billowed around her body.

"...I...can't lose...here!"

She stomped her foot, crushing the head of the frigid construct biting down on her limb. She then used her superhuman strength to leap up. Riselia loosed a few quick slashes and reduced the other Frost Wolves to powder.

"Wh-what...? What is this...?!" Fenris exclaimed in shock. Plumes of cold air rose from her Freezing Knuckles as they closed in. Riselia's sword deftly deflected the punches, though.

"I've always...looked up to you. I always struggled to keep up with you...!"

"...?!"

Riselia's Bloody Sword began to glow a crimson shade. For so long, she had been the girl who had failed to be a Holy Swordswoman. She had yearned for years to be a knight and protect those in need, but she had never awakened to the power of a Holy Sword. That had all recently changed, however.

Now, Riselia was a Holy Swordswoman, pursuing her rival to greater heights. Even if no one expected anything of her, she never stopped trying. Through sneers and biting remarks, Riselia persevered.

My expectations for her weren't misplaced. Leonis confidently nodded to himself.

A Vampire Queen was the highest-ranking member of the undead hierarchy. While that was significant, it was wrong to attribute today's victory solely to it. The true source of Riselia's strength was her iron will.

Riselia's Bloody Sword smashed Fenris's Freezing Knuckles.

"This is my minion. My right-hand woman," Leonis muttered proudly.

◆

"Lady Selia, you were so, so, so amazing! We beat the eleventh platoon! That's the biggest turnabout in the academy's history since...since it was founded!"

The eighteenth platoon was gathered in the corridor of a

massive facility built alongside the training field. Regina had wrapped Riselia up in a hug and was cheering with excitement.

"I didn't do this alone. We won together." Riselia embraced Regina back with a gentle smile on her face.

Taking the opposing team's flag and knocking out their leader, Fenris, had given the eighteenth platoon enough points to win the training match. This was a crowning moment for Riselia and the others.

The next battle was already beginning on the field, so the group made their way to the Undine bathhouse to relax and celebrate their victory.

"Besides, we shouldn't let this win go to our heads. If Fenris hadn't been so fixated on beating me and stayed at her original position, we wouldn't have won."

"You're so serious, Lady Selia...," Regina said, finally releasing her friend from another hug. "But really, this is a huge victory for us. Maybe they'll install a Jacuzzi in our dorm."

"Before they do that, I'd like for them to fix the air conditioner in the living room," Riselia replied with a shrug.

"I'm sorry, everyone. I walked right into the enemy's trap," a blue-haired girl muttered, her shoulders dropped apologetically. It was Sakuya Sieglinde. She wore the Sakura Orchid's traditional garb over her Excalibur Academy uniform.

"No, Sakuya, you did well," Riselia replied.

"That's right. They may have lured you into the forest, but you beat their trap expert all on your own," a slightly older, black-haired girl walking beside them added encouragingly. This was Elfiné Phillet, the eighteenth platoon's operator, and the team's dependable older sister, as it were.

"That was just a fluke. I was hunting down Fenris's wolves when I ran into her. I was just lucky."

"No, if anything, she was unlucky to run into you," Elfiné corrected.

When it came to melee combat, few students could match Sakuya.

"Aww, I wish I got a chance to shine, too," Regina grumbled.

"If you ask me, your mere presence at our base was a big deterrent. The other side's attackers had to tread cautiously," Riselia said.

"Well, if they'd tried anything, I'm confident I would've been able to shoot them down."

"And you beat the archer, Leo." Riselia then turned around to face Leonis. "Congratulations on your first win in a training match."

"I only pulled that off because you had her distracted, Miss Selia." Leonis shrugged and shook his head. "All I did was take advantage of the opening you made for me."

Honestly, I hadn't planned on defeating any of them.

Still, Leonis had been powerless to resist showing off in front of his favorite minion—a bad habit from his Dark Lord days.

"Maaan. I'd have loved to see Leo fight," Regina said enviously. "Elfiné, can you show me the Eye of the Witch recording later?"

"No problem. Oh? Actually, wait a second," Elfiné replied, her expression turning serious for a moment as she activated her communication terminal. "Sorry, my cat's calling for me. I'll meet up with you later, okay?" Elfiné brought her palms together in apology and jogged down the corridor.

"...A cat?" Leonis cocked his head.

"Yeah, Elfiné takes care of a cat," Riselia said. "Apparently, it gets lonely rather quickly, so caring for it has been difficult."

"I haven't seen any felines around the dorm, though," Leonis remarked.

"It walks around academy premises. Elfiné lets it roam free most of the time," explained Riselia.

"Oh, that reminds me, I've heard you started raising a stray dog recently, Sakuya," Regina interjected.

"No, I'm not looking after Fluffymaru the Black..."

It was then that Leonis felt a tug on his sleeve.

"You're coming this way, kid," Regina instructed.

"...Huh?" the Dark Lord managed through his surprise.

"I mean, you're still just ten, right?" Regina said, pointing her thumb in the direction of the girls' bath. "Academy regulations say that children aged ten or less have to bathe with their guardians."

"W-wait, I...!" Leonis tried to protest.

"She's right, Leo," Riselia added. "I'm worried about you bathing alone. You might break something in the bath."

"I won't!" Despite his protestation, Leonis had broken a shower once because he hadn't known how to use it.

"Besides, you always take quick rinses when you go in alone. Your hair's full of sand today, so I want to make sure it's all washed out."

"H-huh? W-wait, Miss Selia, I...!"

"Okay, kid, no more tantrums." Regina chuckled devilishly as she pushed Leonis toward Riselia.

"Grrrr...!" Leonis grumbled as he was all but dragged into the girls' bath.

◆

A layer of white steam hung over the interior of the Undine bathhouse. It was an elliptical structure equipped with multiple facilities, including a sauna, a cold bath, and a steam room.

The polished tile wall sported a design that depicted natural landscapes from before the Void invasion.

And in one corner of this veritable paradise...

"Your skin is so clear, kid!"

"Leo, stop thrashing!"

How did my life come to this?!

Having been stripped naked by Riselia and Regina, Leonis was seated on a bathing stool, absolutely at his wit's end. The warmth in his cheeks was due to far more than hot water.

"We can't wash you if you're curled up like that, kid. Okay, up we go!" Regina, who had undone her pigtails to let her hair down, grabbed Leonis's arms and lifted them.

"...?!"

The Dark Lord could feel wet skin press against his back. A shiver ran through his body as Regina pulled his arms up.

"Hee-hee. What's the matter, kid? Embarrassed?"

"M-Miss Regina, I can...I can wash myself...," Leonis tried his best to reply, but his voice was so meek and flustered that the sound of running water drowned it out.

I... I am a Dark Lord... A Dark Lord who led legions of the undead, ten thousand strong...! Leonis tried to muster his willpower, reminding himself desperately of his mighty status.

Scrub, scrub. Scrub, scrub, scrub.

A sponge gently rubbed against his skin, covering his body with soap bubbles.

"Regina, his body's clean already," Riselia said.

"Okay, okay. I gotcha, Lady Selia," Regina replied. She finally took a step back from Leonis, who breathed a large sigh of relief. Unfortunately, the reprieve was short-lived.

"Leo, close your eyes. You don't want to get shampoo in them."

This time, Riselia's dainty fingers started rinsing his hair. Her fingertips felt oddly cold, likely because she was a vampire.

"Erm... Listen, I can do it myself..."

"No," Riselia turned him down flatly. "You're not thorough enough."

"Ugh..."

Back when Leonis had been the Undead King, he hadn't bathed. Instead, he would just sleep in a coffin. Consequently, he'd pretty much forgotten how to wash himself.

"Your hair's a little frizzy, Leo," Riselia whispered, clearly enjoying herself as she lathered foamy shampoo and rubbed it on his head. "Tell me if there are any itchy spots, okay?"

"I-I'm...fine...," Leonis replied, swallowing nervously.

I hate to admit it, but this cleansing does feel pleasant. It was a sweet numbness that lulled Leonis into a peaceful sleep.

"Sakuya, let me wash your back—" Regina, who had been left with nothing to do, moved behind Sakuya.

"No, I-I can handle myself—"

Sakuya, who was usually casual and indifferent, refused her suggestion with unusual bashfulness.

"...? Oh, Sakuya..." Regina smirked mischievously. "Did your...?"

And then...

"Aaaaah?!"

Regina grabbed onto Sakuya's breasts from behind.

"I knew it. They got a little bigger again. My hawk eyes don't lie, girl."

"...Aaaah, that's not... R-Regina, you...idiot!" Sakuya, her face red, rained playful blows on Regina.

"Don't you agree, Leo?" asked Regina.

"Huh?"

At the question, Leonis raised his face, jolting up from his nap.

Before he knew what was happening, he saw Sakuya's chest hidden behind a thin layer of soap.

"...!" Sakuya let out a wordless scream. She quickly covered her front with a bath towel, her face rosy.

"I-I'm sorry!"

"...H-he...s-saw my...saw my chest..."

"No, it's, erm... You're very...pretty, so..."

"...You!" Pouting her lovely lips, Sakuya glared at Leonis reproachfully. She swiftly pulled a towel from the top of a rack and wrapped it around Leonis's eyes.

"M-Miss Sakuya, what are you—?"

"You might be a kid, but this is... This is still too indecent!" Sakuya regained her composure and tied the cloth tightly around Leonis's head.

"Sakuya, you don't have to worry. It's just Leo. It's fine. Right, Leo?" Riselia pressed, leveling a heavy question at him.

"I—I don't mind! Keep my eyes covered, please!" Leonis nodded desperately.

◆

An angel with wings as black as night soared down, descending into a darkness surrounded by countless grids.

It was the quasi-network produced by mana particles—the Astral Garden.

This virtual space that linked the Assault Gardens was created sixty-four years ago by the Human Integration Project. It was initially a highly classified military secret, but it had been disclosed to the academies in recent years.

Of all the places in this dying world, the Astral Garden was the sole one beyond the Voids' reach. And in this world defined by a grid of light, she could move freely. She wore a sensual dress with a plunging V-neck. Anyone who knew her usual demure conduct would be struck speechless if they saw her now.

She was the queen of the night—Elfiné Phillet. This was her other self, the face she never showed at the academy. Basking in the sense of freedom, she landed upon one of the grids.

"Come on out, Cait Sith," she called out.

A black cat appeared before her and mewed in greeting. This creature, Cait Sith, was Elfiné's personal Artificial Elemental, one that existed in the network. Elfiné had created it by refining one of the orbs from her Holy Sword, Eye of the Witch.

It was this Artificial Elemental cat that had called for her earlier. Apparently, the Phillet Company's headquarters in the Imperial Capital had discovered some suspicious data in the network.

The Phillet Company was the leading authority in producing magical apparatuses, as well as research on and production of Artificial Elementals.

The spirit used in the terrorist attack was one of the Phillet Company's creations.

Typically, the only one who could control the *Hyperion*'s spirit was Princess Altiria. But the spirit the Demon Sword wielders had brought aboard successfully usurped control over the vessel. Regina, who drew on the royal family's blood, had managed to regain control of the ship, but if she hadn't, the *Hyperion* would have charged straight into a Void reef.

If those Demon Sword users are somehow connected with the house of Duke Phillet...

Elfiné had researched the matter for the last few days and discovered some unclear movement of funds within the Phillet Company. However, she hadn't been able to learn anything more precise than that. A powerful barrier guarded the central, top-secret sector.

Cait Sith meowed at Elfiné, and a black cube manifested in front of her.

"That's the suspicious data?" Elfiné leaned forward and carefully poked the cube's surface. The object unraveled in a geometric pattern, and the information condensed within the shape flowed into Elfiné's mind. Within that torrent of data, she found a secured, locked file name.

"...D Project?" Elfiné read dubiously.

D Project. What did the D stand for?

I've got a terrible feeling about this...

Suddenly, a cacophonous alarm blared inside Elfiné's head.

...An urgent call? At a time like this...?

Elfiné hurriedly cut off her connection to the Astral Garden.

"..."

She doffed the small headgear she'd placed over her head and let her sleek black hair flow behind her. Using her fingers to brush her disheveled locks down, Elfiné heaved a small sigh. She was in Excalibur Academy's information control room, a unique facility that used a large, military-grade data terminal.

The school recorded all access to the network, but the Eye of the Witch allowed Elfiné to easily cloak her activities.

An urgent contact from the administration bureau? What's this all about?

Brow furrowed in suspicion, Elfiné looked down at the terminal sitting on the table. Immediately, her eyes widened with shock.

"...What?!"

♦

Scrub, scrub. Scrub, scrub.

"You don't have to be so stiff, Leo," Riselia said with a wry smile from her spot behind the Dark Lord.

"...!" Leonis thought being blindfolded would put him at ease, but he soon realized how major a mistake that was.

The sound of breathing tickled his ears. The sensation of soft fingertips against his body made jolts of pleasure run through his nerves. "Khh... Ahh..." He exhaled in hard gasps despite himself. Having his vision cut off made his other senses that much keener.

"Are you okay, Leo? Does it hurt somewhere?" Riselia's voice implored.

"I-I'm... I'm fine..."

"Hee-hee. What, is it so dark your imagination's working overtime, kid?" Regina chuckled and blew into Leonis's ear.

Boing, boing.

Leonis also felt something decisively soft press against his forearm.

"M-Miss Regina, stop teasing... Haaah... Ahh..."

"Ah, you just moaned like a girl. So cute."

You're doing this on purpose, you blasted maid!

Leonis whimpered, trapped in the ebon of blindness.

"Next, I'll wash your front, Leo."

"M-M-Miss Selia?!" Leonis stiffened as if a petrification curse had just been placed on him.

Before anything could happen, however, a communication terminal started ringing. It was one of the earring devices Riselia wore.

"An urgent summons from the administration bureau? What's happened?" Riselia whispered, her fingers stopping along Leonis's back.

THIRD ASSAULT GARDEN

13:00 Imperial Standard Time.

Having received an emergency request, Riselia and the eighteenth platoon hurriedly changed into their uniforms and arrived at the entrance to Excalibur Academy's Anti-Void Tactical Conference Room.

"Riselia Crystalia, here at your urgent summons," the argent-haired girl stated at the door.

"Come in."

Riselia opened the door. Inside, she saw the eighteenth platoon's instructor, Diglassê, along with Elfiné and a female information analysis officer clad in a knight's uniform. All three were already seated. Elfiné raised her head and nodded gently at the rest of her group's arrival. Diglassê, meanwhile, jerked her chin, gesturing for them to take a seat quickly.

What has happened? Have more Voids appeared? Sensing the unusual air in the room, Leonis took a seat between Riselia and Regina. The eighteenth platoon's girls exchanged puzzled, unsure glances.

"Firstly, there's something I'd like for you all to see," Diglassê stated quietly.

The information analysis officer nodded and fiddled with a device. A large, poor-quality image was projected on the broad meeting table. It depicted some part of the ocean covered with thick, gray fog.

"This is footage taken this morning by an observation unit deployed at the isle of Hakura."

"Hakura? The base there is meant to gather information on the nearby Void territory, right?" questioned Riselia.

That's the first I've heard of that, Leonis thought. "Void territory?" he asked.

"An area filled with a high density of Void reefs," Riselia explained. "They're cursed places that humans can't enter. There's constantly a thick layer of miasma over a Void territory, so ships and tactical fighter planes can't enter or observe what goes on in them."

"While we don't know what occurs within them, we do monitor their outer circumference. The Integrated Empire has set up observation bases on the islands surrounding this Void territory, and they continually monitor that portion of the sea."

I understand. So the Void reef the Hyperion *encountered the other day was like a small, localized version of a Void territory.*

"Today at zero four zero four hours, the observation unit caught signs of a large structure...," Diglassê said, pointing at the image and tapping it with her finger.

When she did, something came into view in the footage. A giant shadow was drifting on the ocean's surface. The sun rose in the recording, revealing the full form of the thing bobbing on the water. A group of artificial islands linked by bridges—but they were dilapidated and lined with the ruins of countless buildings.

"...Is that...?!" Riselia swallowed nervously.

Regina, Sakuya and Elfiné's eyes widened in shocked disbelief.

"It's hard to see clearly because of the miasma, but...," Diglassê began grimly, "after disappearing into a Void territory six years ago, it seems that the Third Assault Garden has returned."

"...?!"

An eerie silence settled over the meeting room.

The Third Assault Garden? If Leonis recalled correctly, that was Riselia's birthplace, a city destroyed in a Void Stampede.

"The Third Assault Garden's mana furnace should have completely shut down," Riselia said, her voice shaking. "And the whole city had to be abandoned. So how...?"

"The cause is still unknown," the information analysis officer replied. "Excalibur Academy speculates that the deactivated mana furnace was driven to an uncontrollable state via some unidentified factor."

"An uncontrollable state...? Is that even possible?" Riselia muttered.

"We haven't seen any cases of this in the past, but that's not to say it's impossible," Diglassê replied. "The fact of the matter is that the Third Assault Garden is currently moving at fourth combat speed."

"Where is it heading?" Elfiné inquired.

"We don't know for certain, but it's been moving steadily south..." Another image appeared over the table at the information officer's command. This time, it was a map showing the portions of the seas under humanity's control. "Which means it will come into contact with the Seventh Assault Garden."

"...!" The girls of the eighteenth platoon exchanged startled looks.

"It's moving slowly, and this is just an approximation, but it should reach us within fourteen days," the information analysis officer concluded.

"Why here?" Elfiné wondered again.

"That is still in the dark, I'm afraid. However..." The officer hesitated for a moment. "Soon after the Third Assault Garden emerged from within the Void territory, it sent two distress signals to the Seventh Assault Garden."

"What?!"

"I-it can't be...," Riselia whispered, an expression of utter shock on her face. "I mean, there shouldn't be anyone there... No one else survived."

"Officially, yes. The only ones who lived through that Stampede were a small group of people who took cover in the underground shelters, including the two of you. But even if there were any undiscovered survivors, they couldn't possibly have endured six years in the Void territory. Yet, something sent those distress signals. There's the possibility of a mechanical malfunction, but..."

"..."

While everyone else was listening to Diglassê's explanation, Leonis's eyes were glued to the image of the ruined city projected on the table. No one but him seemed to notice. More specifically, Leonis was the only one who could have recognized the oddity.

What he saw was...

How? How did that get there? As Leonis pondered a question he could not find the answer to, Diglassê rose from her seat silently and glanced around the room, eyeing everyone present.

"So, with this being the situation, I'm sure you understand the reason I've called you here."

"You want us to investigate the Third Assault Garden," Riselia reasoned.

"Precisely. Eighteenth platoon, I am hereby ordering you to inspect this ruined city."

This didn't come as a surprise. Riselia and the other girls' expressions didn't waver at all. Teens though they were, these young women were students of Excalibur Academy and full-fledged military knights. As bearers of Holy Swords, they accepted their duty and were willing to lay down their lives to protect their home.

"In the event that you encounter a critical situation, you have the approval to retreat at your platoon captain's judgment. Based upon your report as the advance force, the academy will send a larger search party at a later date."

"Have any Voids been sighted in the Third Assault Garden?" Sakuya inquired, speaking for the first time in this meeting. "Considering the city emerged from a Void territory, isn't there a high possibility that it serves as a Void nest?"

"At present, no Void outbreaks have been detected around the target area. But keep in mind that we haven't been able to observe the Assault Garden in detail."

"Excuse me, I have a question," Riselia interjected as she gingerly raised her hand.

"You have permission to speak."

"Serving as an advance force in this situation is an important duty. Why give it to us?"

So far, the eighteenth platoon had been entrusted with refugee rescue and site investigation missions. More important assignments were always given to higher-ranked groups.

Diglassê hesitated before at last replying, "It was the administration bureau's idea. I'm sure a girl as bright as you can understand the meaning behind the choice."

"...It's because I'm Duke Crystalia's daughter, isn't it?"

"Lady Selia..." Regina bit her lips.

Leonis quickly picked up on the situation. *They're saying they want a hero. Humans never change, do they?* he thought bitterly.

Riselia was a tragic girl whose Holy Sword awakened after a long period of dormancy. Bound by the duty of a Holy Swordswoman, she would return to her birthplace, a city destroyed by Voids. Such a beautiful story was bound to grip one's heart no matter what era it was.

One thousand years ago, there was a boy who served as a certain kingdom's hero—Leonis Shealto. His battles brought hope to the people but threw him into despair as he lost agency over his own life.

The current exchange reminded him of that trifling story.

"I won't deny there is political significance to this. However, I do greatly value your strength as a group. Your victory in the practice match this morning was quite impressive."

"Thank you very much, ma'am." Riselia nodded with a resolved expression and looked around, examining her friends' faces.

Regina, Sakuya, and Elfiné each bobbed their own heads in assent.

"Leo..." Riselia's expression wavered when her eyes settled on Leonis's face.

"Yes, he's only ten years old and hasn't been in the academy for long. It's fine if you exclude him from the—," Diglassê started, but Leonis cut her off.

"There's no need to worry about me, ma'am," he said.

"Leo..."

"Miss Selia, I'm part of the eighteenth platoon, too," Leonis reminded, gazing straight into her eyes.

"...Understood. I'll make sure to keep Leo safe," Riselia declared.

Leonis cracked a wry smile. Riselia had witnessed a sliver of his power as a Dark Lord. Even still, she could only see him as a child. That hadn't changed since the day she'd saved him in the mausoleum.

"The eighteenth platoon acknowledges and accepts your orders, ma'am. We will return with results in hand."

Riselia raised a fist over her chest and saluted the instructor.

♦

They were set to sortie four hours later, at seventeen hundred Imperial Standard Time. It was very short notice, but considering the squad's target was on the move, the faster they investigated, the better.

"Make sure to check your equipment thoroughly and individually. Your gear can save your life."

Riselia was in her room in the Hræsvelgr dorm, stuffing her bag with things for the mission.

"Oh, these rations aren't expired yet. We should probably eat them as soon as we can..."

Leonis shrugged as he watched her go about her tasks in a fidgety manner. The entire capital of the Realm of Shadows resided within Leonis's shadow. Shary watched over his treasury and the bones he used to make his skeleton soldiers. He didn't need to bother putting his things into his bag. Thus, Leonis simply sat on the edge of the bed, watching Riselia work.

"And a canteen and a hair dryer... Ah, wait, that won't fit inside, will it?"

She's shaken up. Well, it's easy to see why. After a small sigh, Leonis said, "That city—the Third Assault Garden—that's your birthplace, right?"

"...Yeah." Riselia nodded, her hands stopping. A short silence hung between the two. "...I had a dream this morning," Riselia whispered abruptly.

"A dream?"

"Yeah. About what happened six years ago. It'd been a long time since I last had that dream..." Riselia closed her bag's zipper and turned to face Leonis. "The Stampede that destroyed the Third Assault Garden happened six years ago. I was still only nine, and all I could do was sit in the shelter with Regina and cower. My father was fighting the Voids outside, and I just listened and trembled."

Riselia's shoulders shook as she thought back to that nightmarish day.

"After that, we were lucky enough to be saved by the Seventh Assault Garden's refugee search party, but everyone else had been lost. We couldn't even bury our loved ones." Riselia's words felt distant, and they were tinged with pain.

I see. Survivor's guilt. Riselia was bogged down by a regret she shouldn't have to carry, but that irrational emotion was one Leonis was familiar with. *"I escaped again." That's what you're thinking, right?*

"I have a duty to go back to that place. Honestly, I'm anxious about it, and I don't know what might happen, but..."

"...I know." Leonis nodded.

Suddenly, the communication terminal rang out.

"Elfiné..."

"Selia, I analyzed the route to our destination. Could you give it a look?"

"Ah, yes, of course. I'll be right over," Riselia replied seriously. "I'll be going out for a bit, Leo. Pack up the rest, okay?" With that, the argent-haired young woman hurried out of the room.

"..."

After seeing the door close and confirming that Riselia's footsteps were growing distant...

"Blackas, Shary," Leonis said.

"Did you call, my friend?"

"D-did... *Cough, cough...* Did you call for me, my lord?"

Leonis's shadow rippled, and a large ebon wolf surfaced from within it. A few seconds later, an adorable girl dressed in a maid's uniform appeared after the beast. The black-haired maid was holding a half-eaten doughnut and had her white cheeks stuffed like a squirrel. Her face was dirty with crumbs.

"What is this, Shary?" inquired Leonis.

"Sticky doughnuts. I bought quite a few of them."

"..." Leonis stared at Shary, his eyes narrowed.

"I've got a few for you, too, my lord."

"...Mm."

Shary pulled out a doughnut from one of her sleeves. Leonis took it and bit into it, glaring at the girl all the while.

"Hmm, this is..."

It did have a sticky, unusual texture dissimilar to any other sweet Leonis had eaten so far. The scent of cinnamon made it quite delicious.

"Hmm, this texture... Human civilization truly has come far," Leonis praised.

"Shall I brew you some tea, my lord?" Shary offered.

"Why, yes... Wait, no, there's no need. You really have gotten used to this world, haven't you?" the Dark Lord observed, half-impressed and half-amazed.

"Yes, I've taken up a part-time job in the interest of gathering intelligence."

"Of what sort, exactly?"

"Work involving making sweets," Shary answered, holding a hand up to her chest reverently.

"You are my minion. I don't recall approving anything of

the sort," Leonis stated, pressing a palm to his forehead in exasperation.

"But I can't use the Dark Lords' Armies' funds..."

"Ugh. No, I suppose you can't..."

Leonis's army was critically lacking in funds. His treasure vault in the Realm of Shadows contained many coins that were virtually worthless in this era. They could perhaps be sold as antiquities, but if Leonis were to peddle any mythology-class artifacts from millennia ago, their authenticity could be called into question, which ran the risk of exposing his identity.

"Hmph. Very well," Leonis decided after a few moments, wiping his mouth with a handkerchief Shary offered him. "I want you two to see this."

Holding up the Staff of Sealed Sins, Leonis used his sorcery. The gemstone sitting on the staff's tip, the Dragon's Eye, flashed blue and began replaying images on its pearly surface—namely, the footage of the Third Assault Garden sailing along the ocean.

"What is this?" Blackas asked.

"I'm projecting my memory. This is a massive fortress of the same model as this city. Six years ago, it was destroyed by those despicable Void monsters."

"Hmm. And?"

"Look at this." Leonis held the staff over Blackas's nose. "There, in the plaza near the city's center. Can you see it?"

"...Is that...?!" Blackas's golden eyes widened.

This was what Leonis had noticed earlier in the meeting room, what everyone else had overlooked. It was only natural that they would have, of course, because none among them knew its importance.

However, Leonis had been immediately drawn to it. Red symbols were scrawled on the ground around the plaza. One was a star and the other, a burning eye.

"The Holy Sect's symbol..." Blackas growled.

The Holy Sect was a religious organization that worshipped the Luminous Powers and possessed powerful influence over the human nations one thousand years ago. Much like the gods, the Dark Lords, and the Six Heroes, knowledge of them should have been long forgotten.

So why was their symbol drawn in the ruins of a destroyed city?

The markings couldn't have been made before the Assault Garden was destroyed, because they were clearly etched over the rubble.

"How puzzling. It feels strange that only their symbol would survive the many years," Blackas remarked.

"Indeed. Which makes this our sole clue regarding all that lost history. Perhaps it could even lead us to something connected to Roselia's vessel. To that end..." Leonis brandished his staff, dismissing the image displayed on the jewel. "I will investigate the ruined city. Blackas, my apologies, but..."

"Yes, I understand." Leonis's lupine comrade nodded composedly, as if to imply that no further word was needed. "I shall watch over your kingdom in your absence."

"Please. You're the only one I can trust with this."

Dáinsleif had designated the Seventh Assault Garden as Leonis's domain. As such, he couldn't callously depart it without leaving protection. The remnants of the Sovereign Wolves had only just been inducted into the Dark Lords' Armies and still needed to be carefully monitored before they could be trusted not to do anything untoward.

"My lord, what of—?"

"Shary, you come with me."

"By your will, my lord." Shary bowed her head respectfully.

"Do be careful, Lord Magnus," Blackas said.

"Yes. By the way..." Leonis furrowed his brow, his gaze fixed on Blackas's neck. "I've meant to ask. What's that?"

Clasped around Blackas's neck was a collar with a blue ribbon tied to it.

"A gift from the swordswoman," declared Blackas, showing off the ribbon under his throat.

"Swordswoman...? You mean Sakuya Sieglinde?"

"Yes, her. She said that if I was to walk through the woods on the academy's premises, the humans might mistake me for a stray and make an attempt to hunt me down. Wearing this collar would dispel that suspicion, it seems."

"I see..."

Blackas displayed the accessory with a hint of pride. Leonis felt inclined to ask if it was the sort of thing a royal ought to be wearing, but he held his tongue.

I am certainly in no position to judge. Recalling the incident in the bathhouse, Leonis heaved a small sigh.

◆

"There's no doubting it. *She's* here..."

There stood a girl.

She gazed down at the ruined cityscape from atop the roof of a dilapidated house. Her verdant hair, tied back in a ponytail, wavered slightly in the sea breeze. Excepting her shorts, the young woman's attire appeared wholly foreign. Her blue eyes were as clear as a lake's surface, and the blade of the sword she gripped glinted sharply.

Her petite build spoke to an age of twelve, or perhaps thirteen. However, because of her half-elf heritage, she was actually over twenty years old.

Arle Kirlesio was an apprentice to Shardark Ignis, renowned as a Dark Lord Slayer, and the Swordmaster of the Six Heroes.

The Sanctuary's Elder Tree foretold the Goddess of Rebellion's resurrection.

Arle's slender, elongated ears twitched gently. This city had no signs of life, to say nothing of human activity. It was a place of metal and concrete, a forest all too different from her homeland.

What reduced this place to such a state? the girl wondered to herself.

Was it the Dark Lords, who had brought ruin and devastation to the world one thousand years ago? No, it couldn't have been them. The eight who served the Goddess of Rebellion had already perished.

That meant it had to have been those distorted monsters that appeared from tears in space. The invaders from the hollow darkness that hadn't existed in Arle's time, those so-called Voids. What were those horrible, disfigured creatures? This world had changed too much for Arle.

In the thousand years I've spent slumbering, everything has changed...

The half-elf took in her surroundings as she tightened her grip on her weapon. Arle's blade was the Demon Smiting Sword, Crozax, one of the Arc Seven, the Dark Lord-slaying weapons granted by the Sanctuary's Elder Tree. A weapon made to destroy the Goddess of Rebellion's vessel, which had incarnated in this era.

Suddenly, Arle's ears shivered, picking up on some unnerving presence.

"Ah. I wondered who it might be, but if it isn't the little elf hero."

"...?!"

Swiftly turning around, Arle found that a young man clad in priestly attire had appeared out of thin air. He was slender and looked to be in his twenties. He stood atop the ruins, his blue eyes smiling and alabaster locks wavering in the open air.

He knows who I am? Arle glared at the man. No one in this era should've known she had awakened. Arle felt herself breaking into a cold sweat. *I couldn't even sense his presence. This is no ordinary human...* Her grip on the sword's hilt tightened.

"...Are you the guardian of the Goddess's vessel?" Arle asked, holding up her sword.

The man's lips curled up into a sardonic smile. "'Guardian'? Yes, I suppose that title befits me well enough. Let us assume that I am. What would you do?"

"I will cut you down!" Kicking hard off the ground, Arle leaped into the air and swung down her Demon Smiting Sword mid-jump. However...

"...?!"

Her breakneck slash caught nothing but air. The slender man's visage wavered like a mirage.

"An illusion...!"

"It pains me to turn down a guest, but I'm afraid Dark Lords and heroes have no place in a world filled with Voids." The man's voice echoed on the wind. "I ask that you relinquish the stage."

And the next moment...

Crack... Crack... Crack...!

Accompanied by the sounds of shattering glass, large fissures ran through the air around Arle.

"This is...!"

It was the phenomenon that heralded the appearance of those distorted monsters.

"You...summoned those creatures? Who are you...?!" the half-elf demanded.

"I am Nefakess. Nefakess Void Lord." The introduction's words quickly faded away, and the arm of a large angel crept from the cracks in the air.

◆

Just as the sun was setting over the horizon, the eighteenth platoon boarded the tactical fighter Lindwyrm Mk.III, which launched from Excalibur Academy's third military port. The Lindwyrm Mk.III was one generation older than the Knight Dragons Leonis had destroyed aboard the *Hyperion*.

This wasn't to imply the academy made light of the eighteenth platoon's mission. Rather, it was that the royal family's private vessel was outfitted with cutting-edge prototypes that hadn't been made available for everyday military use yet.

"How do you like sitting in a fighter jet?" Elfiné, who was piloting the plane, asked.

Floating around her were orbs that displayed various glowing symbols. They were Elfiné's Holy Sword, the Eye of the Witch. She used it for support when piloting.

"It's convenient. More spacious than I thought," Leonis replied, looking around the vehicle's undecorated interior. He wasn't wrong. For an aircraft, it was quite spacious.

"Boys all love fighter jets, don't they?" Regina remarked from her spot next to Leonis.

"Oh, that's not true. Girls like them, too." Elfiné chuckled. She had a penchant for weapons, as well as magical apparatuses, terminals, and everything mechanical. Leonis noted that Elfiné might get along well with Linze, the younger of two siblings from the orphanage.

My skull dragon is far more dashing and exciting than this bucket of bolts, Leonis thought to himself as he comfortably settled into his seat, his heart burning with an odd sense of rivalry.

The seats were made in rows of three. Leonis, Riselia, and Regina occupied one row. Apparently, Sakuya didn't handle flying very well. She was sitting in a different set of seats while wearing an eye mask and headphones.

That said, the trip is supposed to last ten hours. Sitting for that long is a bit harsh.

Feeling the vibrations under his feet, Leonis sighed. Back when he'd been the Undead King, he never knew fatigue, and in that regard, this human body was quite incorrigible. Leonis's gaze wandered to the landscape beyond the window, and a question popped into his mind.

"Would have thought the Voids maintained control of the skies." The comment was directed at Riselia, who was seated next to him. There were Void reefs all across the ocean. Crossing above them should have been quite perilous.

"Certain Voids, like the wyvern-class ones, could attack, but there are no records of anything like a reef ever manifesting in the air," Riselia explained, holding up an index finger. "Of course, that's not to say the skies are absolutely secure, so we only use aircraft during missions when a Holy Sword capable of long-range attacks like Regina's is available. The plane is equipped with minimal armaments, but honestly, they're only good for peace of mind."

"I see," replied Leonis.

Simply put, the Voids had usurped control of the sea and skies from humanity. In the past, the eight Dark Lords who had plunged the world into terror had held dominion over not only the oceans and air, but also the mountains where the dragons roosted and the illusory village where the spirits were born. Even the land of death had been under their thumb.

Rivaiz Deep Sea had ruled the oceans, and the sky had belonged to Leonis's worthy rival, Veira Greater Dragon.

When the Dark Lords' Armies again arise, I shall retake air and sea from those twisted beings.

Leonis spent some time staring out the window. Sakuya, who had her back leaned against a chair, soon fell asleep. Watching her slumber proved infectious, as Leonis began to feel drowsy as well.

I have been staying up late working on my castle's design.

Leonis had discarded the need to rest when he'd become the Undead King, but now he had a growing boy's body, and it demanded sleep. Ignoring that siren call was difficult; slumber did have a way of being quite pleasant.

"Heh-heh-heh, you feeling tired, kid?" Regina asked, noticing that Leonis was beginning to nod off.

"We've got a while until we reach our objective, so you can go ahead and rest," Elfiné stated from her spot in the pilot's seat.

"Don't you need to sleep, too, Miss Finé?"

"Once we get on a stable course, I'll leave the steering and patrol to my Eye of the Witch and rest for a bit," she explained.

"You can rest your head right here, kiddo," Regina said, tapping on her lap.

"N-no, thank you!"

"No need to be shy. Come hither."

Regina gently cradled Leonis's head and pushed it down onto her thighs.

"M-Miss Regin—!" Leonis felt his cheeks flush. He tried to sit up immediately, but his head was pressed between Regina's soft lap and her breasts, leaving him unable to move.

"...R-Regina, stop that!" Riselia knitted her brow indignantly.

"Hee-hee. Just relax and be at ease," Regina cooed, her breathing tickling into his ear.

A shiver ran through Leonis's body.

"I'll clean your ears. You'll be asleep before you know it."

Regina took a large cotton swab out of her pocket.

"Th-that's not fair. I want to clean Leo's ears, too...," Riselia complained sullenly.

"First come, first serve, Lady Selia," Regina replied nonchalantly, and she inserted the thing into Leonis's ear.

"Ah... Kuh... Nn..." All the tension drained from Leonis's body. Despite himself, a feminine moan escaped his lips.

"Hee-hee. Don't move around too much, kid." Regina's slender fingers held Leonis's chin in place. The golden tips of her pigtailed hair teased the Dark Lord's cheek.

Kuh...! How is this so...so pleasant...?!

The prideful Leonis wished sincerely to protest, but his young body wasn't capable of resisting the pleasure. Resting on a pretty maid's lap, Leonis could only powerlessly writhe amid sublime delight.

CHAPTER 4

THE WRITHING HOLLOW

"—Leo... Leonis..."

Her voice brushed gently against his ear. It was a call most humans shrank away from, believing it to be an invitation into darkness. However, it was a sound of peace and tranquility for this boy—one that tugged at his heart whenever he heard it.

Sleek black hair, as if the dark of night had melted and weaved into locks. Eyes that glittered like falling stars. That was Roselia Ishtaris, the Goddess of Rebellion, who had led the eight Dark Lords in a war against the Luminous Powers.

Every now and then, Roselia had let the boy rest on her lap. And in place of a bedtime story, she would tell him tales of her time beyond the stars, of the ancient myths and the things she saw there.

"Leo. I might not have much time left to remain by your side."

"...Roselia?" The boy thought it strange. Why would she say something like that?

"I don't want that... I-if it's for you, I'd do..."

"I'm sorry. But this is my fate... No. This is my calling." Roselia's white hand gently covered the boy's eyes. "Soon, I will be gone. A thousand years in the future, I will be reborn."

"...The future?"

"Yes. Could you promise you will come find me when that happens? Swear you'll search for me, no matter what form I might take."

"Of course. I will seek you out without fail. Regardless of what you might become."

◆

"...eo... Leo..."

"...Mm..."

Leonis felt someone shake him. Rubbing his bleary eyes, Leonis turned in his sleep.

"Foolish one... You would dare disturb a...Dark Lord's slumber..."

"Leo?"

"Let your painful demise...be the steep price you..."

"Leo, are you talking in your sleep?"

A cold palm touched his cheek.

"...?!"

That was enough to snap Leonis back to the realm of the waking. "...M-Miss Selia?!" he exclaimed as he bolted upright.

Riselia was staring at Leonis with a perplexed expression on her face. Her ice-blue eyes were full of concern. It seemed that, at some point, he'd been put to sleep on her lap.

"I'm sorry I woke you up. You were tossing in your sleep."

"I had Lady Selia switch places with me after a while," Regina explained, stifling a yawn. "You look cute when you sleep, though, kid."

"D-don't tease me...," Leonis grumbled, blushing as Regina poked his cheek playfully.

"And you were saying something about disturbing a Dark Lord's slumber or something..."

"I, erm. I was just talking in my sleep. Don't pay any attention to it!" Leonis hurriedly spat out in a flustered attempt to dodge the topic.

Apparently, he'd revealed something quite damning while unconscious. That was careless of him.

I need to be wary of sleep talking. Leonis then turned his gaze out the window. "Erm, how long have I been asleep?"

The sky was covered in gray clouds, and the sun had begun to rise.

"About eight hours," Riselia replied after examining the clock.

"That long...?"

"I guess my ear cleaning was just that pleasant. Wasn't it, kid?"

"A-and sleeping on my lap was nice, too! Right, Leo?!"

"D-don't drag me into this argument again!"

"Hmm, we should be touching down at the Third Assault Garden's third port in about ten minutes," Elfiné called. "That's the area where the distress signals originated from."

"All right. Sakuya, time to wake up," Riselia shook the only team member who was still sleeping.

"Mm... Sister...?"

"I'm sorry, but I'm not your sister." Riselia lifted Sakuya's eye mask, prompting the young woman to blink at the bright light.

The tactical fighter began its descent, its main wings' thrusters spewing blue flames. Leonis peered out the window. Beneath the layer of dense mist, a massive artificial structure was sailing across the sea.

So that's the Third Assault Garden.

It was so large it was hard to grasp the full size of the construct.

The central area was covered by a thick layer of sea fog, making it difficult to discern what lay beyond. The jet activated its descent boosters and began its landing sequence.

◆

The Third Assault Garden had been one of humanity's final strongholds and an anti-Void fortress. The sizable artificial island was divided into three linked areas. It was only half the Seventh Assault Garden's size in terms of scale, but that was because the Seventh had been erected later on. Before the Stampede, the Third Assault Garden had been home to a population of over five hundred thousand.

The middle area was called the Central Garden. It was connected to a sprawling residential area and a military port. The eighteenth platoon landed in the latter of the two adjoined sections. The ruins of buildings destroyed by the Voids surrounded them.

A thick fog hung over the port, making for poor visibility. Touching down on the rubble, Leonis stretched his stiff body. A suffocating miasma pervaded everything.

This place is thick with the presence of death. It's not unlike Necrozoa...

It was sunrise, but the sky was clouded over, making for a gloomy, melancholic atmosphere. The scent of the countless deceased still wafted in the air. Had this been the world of one thousand years ago, the Assault Garden would have been a place where the undead naturally formed and roamed about freely.

Leonis heard a set of footfalls behind him. Turning around, he saw Riselia looking up at the ruined buildings with a grim expression on her face. Unsure of what to say, Leonis stood still. Regina, Sakuya, and Elfiné got off the plane and locked its doors.

"The miasma is thicker within the city, so we can't move the plane in there," Elfiné said with a shrug.

The noxious vapors would undoubtedly throw off the precise magical instruments the fighter jet used for navigation. The fog also made plain sight unreliable, which meant flying the plane over the city ran the risk of crashing.

"Miss Riselia...," Sakuya began, perhaps intending to ask the platoon leader about their next course of action.

Riselia shook her head, as if to shake off the sentimentality that overcame her, then nodded. "Let's begin the preliminary investigation of the urban area."

Leonis and Riselia would inspect the residential section to the west, while Regina, Sakuya, and Elfiné would handle the east. Riselia and Regina were familiar with the city. Thus, one of each went to the two groups. Riselia had Leonis partner with her, perhaps out of concern that his powers might be exposed if a fight broke out.

She's a smart one. The wise decision only left Leonis feeling even more proud of his minion.

"Take this, Selia," Elfiné said, handing over one of the Eye of the Witch orbs to her.

An ordinary communication terminal wouldn't function in the miasma, so they needed Elfiné's Holy Sword for long-distance communication.

"Don't forget to submit hourly updates, and remember to be careful," Riselia reminded the squad.

"I'm leaving Lady Selia in your care, kid," Regina whispered into Leonis's ear before they parted ways.

"We'll be fine," Leonis replied with a confident nod. He then directed a telepathic message into his shadow.

"Shary."

"Yes, my lord?"

Leonis's shadow writhed a bit as the assassin answered him.

"Escort the three of them."

"**But what about guarding you, my lord?**" Shary asked with a hesitant tone.

Leonis lacked much of the magical power he'd originally had, and his physical prowess was close to nil. Given his current form, Shary's concern was understandable.

"**That will not be necessary. Who do you take me for?**"

"**But...**"

"**I won't repeat myself.**" Leonis glared at his shadow harshly.

"**...My apologies, my lord.**" It looked as if the thing recoiled in fear.

Shary was a ditzy maid, but Leonis trusted in her skills as an assassin. And leaving Regina and the rest in her care gave him some peace of mind.

Me, a Dark Lord, protecting humans... Leonis gave a self-deprecating chuckle. *Well, they're the citizens of my kingdom, after all.* Even as he thought that, some part of Leonis had to wonder if that was really all there was to it.

◆

The wind whistled as it blew through half-crumbled buildings. As Riselia and Leonis trekked over the rubble, their footsteps echoed hollowly around them.

"This was where the Crystalia Knights formed their last line of defense against the Voids," Riselia explained, stepping up in front of a crumbled fortification. She looked around, her silvery hair wavering. There were no signs of movement in the ruined city. "Be careful. The roads might cave in."

"I will. Ah...!" Leonis managed before tripping over a piece of rubble.

Riselia hurriedly caught his arm. "Are you all right, Leo?" she asked.

"...Thank you."

"Don't push yourself too hard. If you're tired, we can take a break." Riselia stopped and surveyed her surroundings. "Everything really is gone."

"..."

All traces of life had been purged. There weren't even bones. *Come to think of it...Voids eat humans.*

When a person was consumed by one of those creatures, they disappeared without a trace, as though erased from existence.

"What about underground? There could be survivors down there," Leonis suggested.

If this city was anything like the Seventh Assault Garden, there had to be a subterranean shelter.

"Yes. The underground safe house should have rations, a seawater filtering device, and a generator. But I still don't think it's likely that anyone has managed to survive in a Void territory for six years..."

Riselia and Leonis continued deeper into the remnants of the former's birthplace. After walking for twenty minutes, they came across a facility that was still mostly intact. It was a large complex consisting of an athletic concourse and multiple short, several-story buildings.

"This was where the school was," Riselia said, her voice shivering slightly.

"Like our Excalibur Academy?" asked Leonis.

"No. This wasn't a place to train Holy Swordsmen. It was a place for ordinary children...," Riselia replied, pushing the broken outer gate open. "It looks like the building is still intact. Let's go inside."

Riselia entered the ruined grounds of the school. Surprisingly, the indoor areas weren't as badly damaged. Riselia advanced through a corridor filled with dust and up a staircase. There'd been an elevator at the end of the hall, but it wasn't active.

"Let's go to the rooftop. We might spot something from a higher vantage point," Riselia suggested.

"...Okay," Leonis accepted.

The pair climbed the steps, covering their mouths so as not to inhale any dust.

Her birthplace, eh...? Leonis thought as he gazed at Riselia's back.

Suffice it to say, Leonis didn't see the Rognas Kingdom, which was where he'd been born, as his native home. If he truly had such a thing, it was Necrozoa, but it had fallen, and all of Leonis's subordinates were long gone. All that felt like home to Leonis now—the one place he belonged—was...

At her side.

Riselia and Leonis reached the fourth floor and found themselves blocked from climbing any farther by a closed shutter.

"Hyahhh!"

However, Riselia used her Vampire Queen power to kick it open.

"Miss Selia, that's violent."

"Mm, I'm sorry. I'm a bit on edge...," Riselia admitted, averting her gaze awkwardly.

"You're still not fully acclimated to your strength, so you might injure your legs without realizing it. Be careful."

The two of them went through the large hole in the shutter and stepped outside. The rooftop had a water tank outfitted with a filtering device and a ration storehouse.

"We should have a good view of things from up here," Riselia said, standing in front of the broken fence that ran the circumference of the top of the school building.

Holding down her silvery hair to keep it from billowing in the wind, Riselia gazed down at what remained of the city. "That's the Central Garden. It's where Regina and I used to live." She pointed to an area connected to this one by a bridge. It was around where Excalibur Academy would be in the Seventh Assault Garden.

"Can you see it?" Riselia asked, narrowing her ice-blue eyes. She then suddenly picked up Leonis by the armpits and lifted him.

"Ah...!" he exclaimed.

"Oh. You're light, Leo."

"Miss Selia, p-put me down!" Leonis demanded in flustered shock, his face going red. That's when he caught sight of something in the distance.

That's...

"...What's wrong, Leo?" Riselia asked, putting Leonis back down on the ground.

"Miss Selia, have you ever seen that pattern over there before?"

"What do you mean...?" Riselia followed Leonis's finger. After spotting the symbol, she shook her head. "No, never. It looks kind of...eerie."

Hmm. Eerie, you say...

Humans from one thousand years ago regarded that mark as something holy. Curiously, it came across as disturbing to the people of this era.

The symbol of a star and a burning eye.

One thousand years ago, the design could be found most everywhere in human territories. It was the mark of the Holy Sect. Leonis had spotted the symbol in a different part of the city during the meeting back at the Seventh Assault Garden. Could the design be carved into places all around the city?

But who would do that...?

"...?!" Sensing something behind himself, Leonis wheeled around.

Crack, crack, crack...!

Numerous fissures ran through the air mere footsteps away from where Riselia and Leonis were standing.

"...Voids!"

"Leo, get back!" Riselia shouted as she took a defensive stance in front of the boy.

The fractures quickly multiplied, looking like a floating, nearly shattered pane of glass. With a terrible sound, Voids smashed through the cracks.

"Grrrrrr... Grrr!"

Humanoid, bipedal abominations that moved as though drifting through the ocean, stepping forward with a ghastly stride. Their skin was pale to the point of transparency, and they gave off a dim glow. Their arms dangled down to the ground. Sharp talons that dripped with viscous mucus adorned every finger.

They look similar to a type of monster that makes its home in the swamps, the Vodyanoy. But no...

"Activate—Bloody Sword!" Riselia called out, holding up her right hand. Particles of light converged in her palm, manifesting into a Holy Sword. Several dozen Voids appeared around the young woman, surrounding her and Leonis, but Riselia glared at them defiantly.

"There's a lot of them," Leonis observed gravely.

"Yes. And I've never seen this type of Void before...!" Riselia nodded, gripping her Holy Sword tightly.

"Raaaaaahhhh!" the humanoid creatures howled. Opening their mouths wide to reveal rows of small fangs, they lunged forward with their claws poised to strike. Leonis quickly called the Staff of Sealed Sins.

"Flamis!" He chanted a third-order spell, the Blazing Heat Wave.

Whoooosh!

Jets of fire shot from the tip of Leonis's staff, reducing three of the Voids to ashes. Their carbonized remains crumbled to the ground.

"Flamis! Flamis! Flamis!"

The Dark Lord loosed more spells in rapid succession, destroying Voids as they crept out of the fissures. The air grew dry and hot. Undaunted, Riselia plunged into the conflagration, enveloped by mana.

"Hrahhh!" Her Holy Sword shone red and cleaved through two Voids at once.

"Leo, fall back for now...!" Riselia called out and turned around.

No sooner had she done so, however...

"Sta... Cry...sta...liaaaaaaa...!"

...Than the Voids she cut down let out moans that almost sounded like words.

"...Huh?" Riselia's blue eyes widened. "What did they just...?!"

Crack, crack, crack, crack!

Unfortunately, before any answer could come, another fissure, this one large enough to swallow the entire building, began to form.

"...Miss Selia!" Leonis called out to warn her. He'd seen a similar phenomenon on the *Hyperion*'s deck.

A large one is coming!

A split second later, the breach widened and exploded outward!

Booooooooooooooooooooom! As if swallowed up by the Void, the ruins of the school crumbled away.

"...?!"

The structure had been brittle to begin with. The building toppled to pieces, drawing its surroundings into a large hole that formed in the ground. The crater was so deep that Leonis couldn't spy its bottom.

What is this?! Some kind of underground hollow...?! Leonis thought as he plummeted down.

He recalled his battle with Arakael Degradios, one of the Six Heroes. There'd been a large shaft beneath the Seventh Assault Garden's surface that had led to some subterranean facility. And the Assault Gardens all shared the same fundamental structure.

As the hole consumed several dozen Voids, Leonis located Riselia among the falling rubble.

"Miss Selia!" Reaching his hands out in midair, Leonis tried to use gravity magic to catch her. But at that moment, another fissure appeared in the air between them. Space itself twisted and cracked as something began to appear—a massive arm, its fingers extending to catch and crush Leonis!

"Tch!"

The Dark Lord dispersed the gravity spell he'd begun to intone and quickly switched over to another attack.

"Farga!"

Vroooooooooooom! An explosion rumbled in front of Leonis. The shock waves rattled the air, blowing his body back.

"Zoh Fia!" Leonis quickly chanted a gravity spell to stabilize himself in midair. "Who in the world is this?! Nng, kah!" Leonis choked as he breathed dust. When things settled, the visage of a giant creature pushing apart the fissure in space became visible.

It was a massive, humanoid statue that dwarfed any of the crumbled buildings. Its surface was like polished marble that surged with lightning. It didn't have a head, and floating above its neck was a rainbow-hued aura.

A gigantic Void, eh? It was the first time Leonis had seen this variety of Void, but it did strike him as familiar in another sense.

Could it be...an apostle of the Luminous Powers...an angel?!

Angels were the servants of the gods and the natural enemies of the undead legions. Their fists could crush mountains, and their spears of holy light could transform any landscape into a sea of flames.

"A Void in the image of an angel, is it?"

Leonis held up his Staff of Sealed Sins. This Void gave off a greater sense of pressure than the humanoid Voids from earlier had.

Where's Riselia...?

Scanning the abyss below, Leonis quickly spotted her. A Vampire Queen could manifest wings of mana to fly, but Riselia wasn't used to handling her power, and Leonis doubted she could do it on the spot.

What manner of madness is this?!

Anger gripped Leonis. He trusted that Riselia's powerful Vampire Queen body could withstand the shock of the fall, but that may have been wishful thinking on the Dark Lord's part. This chasm was so deep as to appear bottomless, after all.

"Selia! Leo! Did something happen?!" Elfiné's voice called. The Eye of the Witch orb she had left with Leonis and Riselia rotated through the air, flying toward Leonis. Elfiné had probably activated it upon hearing the explosions.

"We're fighting a large Void! Miss Selia is—"

"Leo?!"

"Kriiiiiiiiiiiiiiiiiiiiiiiiiiiiiiiiiiiiiiiiiiiii!" The angel let out a horrid, dissonant screech. Its aura rotated as its massive body began emanating some sort of glow.

"...Tch, Rua Meires!" Leonis reflexively deployed a barrier, negating the torrent of light. But Elfiné's orb was caught up in the attack and destroyed. Leonis's shield parted the luminous ribbon of energy, dividing it into two beams that went on to slice through buildings in the distance. In terms of sheer power, it was equal to a fourth-order spell.

"...You irritating cur..." Leonis clicked his tongue.

Angels had high resistance to sorcery from the Realm of Death. In many ways, they were the undead's natural enemy. A mere angel was no match for the Undead King at his full strength, but in Leonis's current body, engaging the creature would prove irksome.

Leonis looked down at the pit below. He wanted to disregard the Void and hurry to his minion's side. However, the angel seemed determined to take Leonis down, as it spread its wings to charge at him.

I should clear this up already. Leonis spun the Staff of Sealed Sins in his hand, thrusting its tip toward his opponent.

"Angel who has succumbed to nothingness, I will show you the essence of true sorcery!"

CHAPTER 5

GHOSTS OF THE RUINED CITY

At the bottom of the dark, enclosed shaft, Riselia wearily cracked her eyes open.

"...Ngh...!"

Her attempt to stand was rewarded with a numbing pain that shot through her legs. Looking down, Riselia realized that the limbs had been slammed against the ground and now bent at unnatural angles.

They're broken, huh? Riselia took in the situation coolly.

Naturally, an average human's body would have been crushed beyond recognition after plummeting from such a height. Riselia was a member of the undead, however—something she was thankful for at this moment.

How far have I fallen...?

Riselia strained her neck, looking around. Unfortunately, even her vampire eyes, graced with superior night vision, could hardly see anything in this darkness. This was a vast, silent place.

It had to be an abandoned shelter. Gigantic roots had torn through the metallic bulkheads, rendering them useless.

Riselia could hear the sounds of Leonis fighting in the

distance. She planted her hands on the ground, trying to push herself up, when suddenly...

"...Huh?!"

Riselia's crimson glowing eyes detected something writhing in the darkness ahead.

◆

"Cut Apart Through Dragon Scales, Demonic Blades of Ice—Sharianos!" Leonis chanted a spell, his mana amplified by the Staff of Sealed Sins. This eighth-order water element magic formed countless ice blades in midair, which rained down on the opponent. But just as they were about to strike the angel-class Void, it let out an unnatural sound. A shield of light formed around it, deflecting Leonis's attack.

Ah, so it has retained its Holy Protection ability...

Holy Protection was a sacred boon granted to high-ranking angels, capable of rendering all spells of the eighth order or below inert. Breaking through this protection wasn't easy. It was why angels, the apostles of the gods, were said to be equal to dragons.

Undoing his gravity control spell, Leonis landed near the shaft's rim. Controlling gravity required a great deal of concentration to regulate one's mana, making it ill-suited for use in the middle of combat.

The floating Void let out another dissonant screech, and a radiant sword formed in its hands. It was a sixth-order holy magic spell, the Punisher's Sword—a lightning attack that had once tormented the Dark Lords' Armies.

"Tch!"

The angel hurled the conjured blade at Leonis, who parried it with the Staff of Sealed Sins, which he'd charged with his mana.

Bzzzzzzzzzzzzzzzzzzzzzt!

The sword of light dispersed, releasing a shock wave that mowed through the surrounding ruins. The ripples sent clouds of dust into the air, obscuring Leonis from sight. The Void began chanting its holy magic again, forming another glowing blade in its hands.

In a matter of moments, six radiant swords floated in the air. With a single motion, the Void unleashed them all at once.

Boom, boom, boom, boom!

Thunderous roars echoed, reverberating all around. The Void flapped its deformed wings, blowing away the dirt and rubble in the air. However, there was no sign of Leonis below.

"Look up, fool."

A giant, winged shadow eclipsed the angel. A skeletal dragon that rivaled the Void in size was soaring up above. Kneeling on its back was Leonis, who sneered down at his opponent scornfully.

"You have no right to look upon a Dark Lord, lowly angel." Leonis then thrust forward the Staff of Sealed Sins and chanted a spell: "Crush All—Beruda Gira!"

Bwoom! A condensed orb of gravitational force knocked the Void down into the ground. Its massive form sank into the earth, forming a large crater.

"Farga! Farga! Farga!"

Leonis fired third-order destructive spells in quick succession, which hit the Void and exploded. The Dark Lord didn't give his opponent time to activate its Holy Protection. The Void spread its wings of light and took off, speeding toward the skull dragon.

"Oh, you are a bulky one, aren't you?" Leonis mocked.

The skull dragon's eye sockets gleamed crimson.

"Graaaaaaaaaaaaaaah!"

It let out a rumbling, ominous roar before sinking its fangs into the Void's arm. Then, it unleashed its Breath of Death, an undead dragon attack capable of rotting the earth and tainting the soul. The fatal vapor had decimated legions on the battlefield.

One of the Void's arms crumbled away, sending the creature plummeting to the ground. Using its other arm, the Void tried to lob a Punisher's Sword at Leonis. However...

"Too slow."

...Leonis had already completed his own incantation.

"Ninth-order spell—Madia Zolf!"

Boooooooooooooooooom!

Hit with a flash of heat capable of melting mithril away, the Void's massive form tumbled limply into the enormous crater.

"And here's one more to remember me by: Rias Gia!"

Without wasting a moment, Leonis quickly intoned another ninth-order spell. Dark bolts of lightning rained down upon the angel-class Void, utterly destroying it.

"A bit too spectacular of a showing for such a weakling," Leonis spat. He then peered down into the abyss below. The skull dragon swooped down, descending into the hole with Leonis perched on its back.

◆

Leonis ventured farther into the depths, using an orb of light to illuminate his way. After flying down several hundred meters, he finally reached the bottom of the shaft. Leonis dismounted the skull dragon and returned it to his shadow.

Lighting a small flame at the tip of his staff, he examined his surroundings. It was a large, circular space. There were tunnels on opposite sides of the chamber, presumably for transporting cargo. Riselia was nowhere to be found.

Leonis furrowed his brow, suspicious, and looked up.

Did she get caught somewhere mid-fall? No...

If she had, Leonis would have spotted her as he rode his dragon down. Searching his surroundings, Leonis spotted speckles of blood on the ground.

"...!" He swallowed nervously despite himself.

The drops were fresh. It must have been Riselia's blood. Increasing the light at his staff's tip, Leonis saw the bloody trail led into one of the adjoining tunnels.

The Dark Lord felt a sense of anxiety grip his heart. A vampire's mana granted them natural regenerative abilities. If Riselia simply stayed put, her injuries would heal on their own. There should have been no reason for her to move.

Could she have been fleeing something? Or was she taken away?

Leonis broke into a run. With drops of crimson as his guide, he dashed into the tunnel with a flame held overhead to light the way.

"...lia! Miss Selia!" Leonis's voice echoed in the empty ebon.

That's when...

"...Le...o! Leo, over here!"

Leonis turned his light in the voice's direction. The shaft connected to that large room Leonis had dropped into appeared to be a large storage space. Inside a room surrounded by concrete walls, Leonis found Riselia sitting on the floor.

"Miss Selia...!"

But as soon as he stepped into the room, Leonis froze in place. There was someone else there. A large group of moving skeletons surrounded Riselia.

"Voids?!" Leonis raised his voice sharply and readied his Staff of Sealed Sins.

"Leo, wait!" Riselia pleaded with a shout. "They're not Voids! These people are—"

"Huh?" Leonis narrowed his eyes dubiously, lowering his staff. The skeletons all turned to face him, their eye sockets alight with a blue glow. And then...

<We are...the ghosts of this ruined city...> They spoke, their solemn voices echoing through the underground space.

❖

"Hahh, hahh, hahh..."

"Are you all right, Miss Elfiné?" Regina asked, turning to face her upperclassman.

Unlike Regina and Sakuya, who had kept up with the academy's basic stamina training, Elfiné was an upperclassman in the information sciences department, and she wasn't great when it came to running.

"Y-yes... I'm fine...," Elfiné replied, panting hard as she continued to dash.

Many of the ruined city's streets were broken and crumbled, and some spots had wholly caved in. The group wouldn't get lost with Elfiné there to lead them, but they couldn't follow the fastest route and had to take significant detours.

Eventually, the three of them arrived at where the school had previously been. But upon seeing what was left, the trio stood stock-still and stunned.

"What...happened here?"

The gigantic Void they'd spotted in the distance wasn't anywhere to be found now. However, the surrounding buildings had all collapsed, and multiple craters had been torn into the ground. Most striking of all, though, was a massive hole that led down into a shaft connecting to the Assault Garden's underground facilities.

Elfiné shook her head silently. Clouds of dust clung to the air, making it hard to see anything. There was no sign of any Voids or Riselia and Leonis.

"It seems the Voids were destroyed. I can't sense their presence," Sakuya said.

"Did Lady Selia and the kid defeat them?" Regina inquired.

"...Who's to say?" Elfiné answered. The orb she'd left with Riselia got destroyed during the battle. Thankfully, the footage prior to its annihilation was stored in the orbs' shared network. It could be extracted, but that would take time.

"Lady Selia! Kid! Where are you?!" Regina called out. She then leaned over the large, gaping shaft.

"Regina, that's dangerous," Elfiné chided her hurriedly.

"They didn't fall down there, did they?" Regina asked, her voice shaking.

"..." Elfiné swallowed nervously. If Riselia and Leonis had indeed plummeted into the pit, the chances of their survival were depressingly low.

"I'll go down and look for them," Sakuya declared, preparing to dive in with Raikirimaru in hand.

"Sakuya, that's insane," Elfiné protested.

"I'll be fine. If I envelop my legs in electromagnetic energy, I should be able to run along the wall—"

"You can do that?" Regina questioned.

"Yes. I mean, I've never done it for real, but it *should* work."

""You can't!"" Regina and Elfiné concurrently shouted just as Sakuya was about to leap right into the chasm.

"Just calm down. I'll send one of my eyes to investigate what's down there," Elfiné said, forming a new orb of light in her hands.

However...

"Miss Elfiné!"

Sakuya pushed the older girl away. The silvery blade of a sword swept across Elfiné's field of vision.

Krrrrrrrrrrr! Metal clashed with a terrible screech, producing a shower of sparks.

What?!

Having fallen to the ground, Elfiné peered through the dust that had been kicked up. Sakuya's Raikirimaru was locked with another girl's blade. She was petite and couldn't have been more than twelve or thirteen. Her verdant ponytail wavered in the wind.

The mysterious girl's attire was foreign to the members of the eighteenth platoon. And her pale, slender arms gripped a sizable double-edged sword that looked far too heavy for her to wield reasonably.

"...Who are you?" Sakuya demanded, her sword still locked with the other young woman's.

"...You speak, monster?!" The girl's eyes widened slightly. "How eerie. Foul creature...!"

Sakuya didn't miss this momentary opening, however, and she struck. The tendrils of electricity running along Raikirimaru's blade only managed to skim along the girl's brow, though, sending a few of her forelocks flying.

She dodged Sakuya's sword?!

But electrical attacks weren't Sakuya's Holy Sword's true power. Lightning enveloped Sakuya's body, accelerating her movements. She swiftly brought her weapon down on her opponent's neck.

"..."

Sakuya stopped her slash at the absolute last moment, standing stock-still. The other girl's blade was fixed against Sakuya's throat, too. Her blue eyes gazed directly at Sakuya.

"Let's stop." Sakuya was the first to lower her sword.

"What...?!" her opponent exclaimed.

"You're strong. I probably would have lost if you were in perfect health."

"...Tch." The girl bit her lip. With one hand, she clutched her abdomen. Drops of blood dripped from a large wound in her stomach. "Who...are you...?" She let out a pained, whispered moan as she crumpled to the ground.

◆

Beneath Leonis's magically conjured light, the distorted skeletons writhed like half-broken toys, casting eerie shadows on the floor.

<We were...the Crystalia Knights...,> a one-armed skeleton said with a crackling voice.

"The Crystalia Knights?" Leonis asked. He knelt down to help Riselia. A clean cloth bandage was wrapped around her right leg. Apparently, these undead had carried her to safety and treated her injuries.

"It was a knight order in service to House Crystalia," Riselia explained. "They fought to defend this city with my father."

<Six years ago... We laid down our lives...fighting the Void Stampede...> The skeletons spoke in time, their voices echoing through the dark room.

So they're wandering dead. Being the Undead King, Leonis quickly realized what these skeletons truly were. At the sites of large clashes, souls that harbored intense, lingering regrets could sometimes remain in the realm of the living.

It wasn't an uncommon phenomenon. During Leonis's reign as a Dark Lord, large numbers of undead would rise after battles had ended even without the use of Realm of Death sorcery.

It seems the people of this age don't know of the undead, though...

Most lands in this era were exhausted of mana, so modern people had never seen undead rising on their own.

But this ruined city is different...

The Voids had brought a vast massacre down upon this place, and it was left untouched for years, surrounded by a miasma. It was no surprise that all the negative mana built up in this place would become a crucible for its wandering spirits.

A Vampire Queen reigned over all undead. The lost souls of the Third Assault Garden had been drawn to Riselia's presence of death.

Leonis placed his Staff of Sealed Sins on the ground and corrected his posture.

These undead were all warriors who had fought to protect their country. Even Leonis, known for his arrogance, abided by a Dark Lord's dignity and knew to respect their bravery.

<Do you...not...fear us...?> the skeletons asked Riselia.

"I'll admit I'm a bit scared of ghosts, but I'm used to skeletons," Riselia answered, reaching out and taking the bony hand of one of her saviors.

<Oooh... Our mistress... Lady...Riselia...> The knights kneeled in reverence.

Riselia had fought plenty of skeleton soldiers during her training with Leonis, so these hardly gave her pause. She gazed into the creatures' dimly lit eye sockets.

"Were you the ones who sent the distress signals to Excalibur Academy?"

<Yes... It appears they reached you...safely...>

Riselia and Leonis exchanged glances. They never expected that mysterious call to have been sent by a group of rogue undead. However...

"Why did you summon us?" Leonis asked.

What could the dead possibly desire?

If they wish for their trapped souls to be set free, I could grant that easily enough.

That was simple for Leonis, who had governed over death. But he doubted they went as far as sending a distress signal to Excalibur Academy just for that.

<...We do not...seek salvation...> One of the skeletons shook its head in denial. <We did it...to warn you...>

"Warn us?" Riselia pressed.

<Yes... If things are allowed to continue... The tragedy of six years ago... A Stampede will consume...the Seventh Assault Garden...>

"What...?!" exclaimed Riselia. "What do you mean? The Void Lord who destroyed our home was said to have disappeared..."

<Not the one...from six years ago...>

<A greater, much stronger Void Lord than the one back then...>

<A new Void Lord...has appeared in these ruins...>

"What...?!"

◆

The knights explained that, fourty-two days ago, a Void in the form of a beautiful woman fused with the massive mana furnace appeared slumbering in the heart of the city, deep beneath the Central Garden.

"Fused with the mana furnace?" Riselia repeated the skeletons' words in disbelief.

I've heard something like this before, Leonis whispered to himself bitterly.

During the Stampede in the Seventh Assault Garden, Arakael Degradios, the Archsage of the Six Heroes turned Void, had attempted to fuse with that settlement's mana furnace.

However, there was something else about what the undead said that caught Leonis's attention.

Forty-two days ago?

That was around the same time Leonis had awoken from his magical hibernation. It felt too eerie for mere coincidence. As Leonis mulled over the meaning of it all, the skeletons continued.

<And...after merging with the city's...core...the Void Lord began...creating its minions of emptiness...>

"Yes, we saw them on the surface. Humanoid Voids that appeared from tears in space."

"I fought a giant, angel-like Void and destroyed it," Leonis appended.

<The large ones are...summoned from the emptiness, but...the humanoid Voids...are different from the others...>

"...What do you mean?"

<They are...the souls of wandering warriors...like us... The Void Lord's power...reduced them to monsters...>

"...What?!" The color drained from Riselia's face. "Are you saying those creatures were...this city's...?!"

"Voids using the souls of the dead like that... Is that possible?" Leonis inquired.

"I... I've never heard of it before." Riselia shook her head, still taken aback.

<...We can...hear its voice...>

"Voice?" Riselia asked the wandering souls.

The spirits began to groan in miserable agony.

<Yes... The call... It tries to tear our souls...away...>

<Ordering us to...fall into the emptiness... A woman's voice...>

<It cannot...be resisted...>

<...Those...near the center...of the mana furnace...were trapped, transformed into Voids...>

<Soon, we too shall...join the ranks of those terrible monsters...>

<To fight eternally...beneath the Holy Woman of the heroes...>

"Holy Woman?" Leonis questioned, latching on to that particular phrase.

"Leo?" Riselia looked at the boy, confused.

"Sorry to cut in. Is that Holy Woman the Void Lord?" Leonis asked, leaning forward despite himself. He knew that title. If this wasn't happenstance, the one it referred to was...

<Yes... The Holy Woman... Tea...ris...>

<Tearis... Void Lord... That's the monster's name...>

Tearis Resurrectia, the Holy Woman. She was the princess priestess once worshipped by the Holy Sect, and a member of the Six Heroes. One thousand years ago, she was one of Leonis's archnemeses.

So Tearis has returned as a Void Lord.

The gods had granted the Holy Woman of the Six Heroes the power of Resurrection. And if she retained that ability as a Void...

Perhaps she can revive the wandering souls as Voids, Leonis theorized, resting a hand on his chin.

Following Arakael Degradios, it seemed that yet another one of the Six Heroes had been brought back after a millennium. It almost seemed to herald the rebirth of the Goddess of Rebellion, Roselia. Once-great heroes were becoming Void Lords who endangered humanity's continued existence.

What in the world is going on? Though he'd been handed more pieces, Leonis still didn't have a complete picture.

"So this Void Lord is trying to cause a Stampede in the Seventh Assault Garden?" Riselia's nervous question yanked Leonis back to the matter at hand.

<Correct... It wishes to...destroy mankind... Return it to... emptiness...>

"But why the Seventh?"

<...We do not...know... The voice...simply orders...>

The skeletal hand Riselia was holding suddenly began to crumble.

"?!"

<It seems...our time has...run out...>

The light in the skeletons' eye sockets was growing dim. Those souls bound to the old bones were beginning to depart.

<We've informed...our human comrades...of the coming danger...>

<Please... Take this information, and return... Leave this place...>

<Before the Void Lord...awakens...>

<The tragedy of six years ago...must not...repeat itself...>

As their voices resounded in the dark chamber, the skeletons crumbled one by one.

"Wait...!" Riselia pleaded.

<Lady Riselia... You have grown to be...so gallant...> Making those its final words, the spirit that had been holding Riselia's hand fell to pieces that dropped to the ground with a dull noise.

CHAPTER 6

THE ELF HERO

"Are you all right? Does it hurt?" Regina asked.

"Ugh..." The girl lying on the ground grimaced.

"I treated the wound, but it still isn't a good idea to move all that much, okay?"

"You seem quite accustomed to this... Are you an apothecary or healer?"

"I'm a maid."

"What is a servant doing in such a place...?" the girl asked quizzically, looking down at her bandaged flank.

"Still, I'm surprised you could keep up with Sakuya in a sword fight with those injures," Elfiné remarked.

The young woman looked a few years younger than the members of the eighteenth platoon. She had bound her green hair back in a ponytail, and her large eyes wavered slightly when she suffered occasional pangs of pain. Her most striking physical feature was her long, sharp ears—a telltale characteristic of elven heritage.

"So," Regina began as she stowed a medical kit, "why did you try to attack us earlier?"

"I thought you were in league with those monsters." The girl averted her gaze, sulking.

"Monsters? You mean Voids?"

"..." The girl nodded silently.

"I know some Voids resemble humans, but..." Elfiné trailed off, bringing her index fingers together in thought.

Some Voids, like the merman and Brain Eater classes, had forms that resembled people, but their outward countenances helped quickly identify them as different sorts of creatures.

"There are Voids that look identical to humans," Sakuya, who had just returned from scouting out their surroundings, commented. "I've seen them before."

"Completely humanlike Voids?" Elfiné furrowed her brow. "Nothing like that has ever been reported."

"No, I'd imagine it hasn't," Sakuya retorted, and then she leaned forward to address the wounded girl. "That injury. Did those Voids do it to you?"

"...Yes," the green-haired girl admitted with no shortage of bitterness over it. "I was careless, and they caught me by surprise."

"What's your name?"

"..." She seemed to hesitate for a moment, but then, "...Arle. Arle Kirlesio."

"Arle. That's a nice name," Sakuya said with a smile.

Arle averted her gaze awkwardly. Elfiné quickly activated one of her Holy Sword's orbs. In response, it began to display a sea of words.

"An elf called Arle... No one matching that description exists in the Seventh Assault Garden's database."

"Were you the one who sent the distress signals to the academy?" Regina questioned.

"What are you talking about?" Arle shook her head and then

turned her own queries to the group. "Who are you people? What are you doing in this place?"

"We're a reconnaissance team dispatched by the Seventh Assault Garden to investigate this ruined city."

Elfiné briefly explained their circumstances. She told Arle of how this floating metropolis had been destroyed six years ago, as well as its mysterious reappearance.

"An Assault Garden...," Arle whispered to herself upon hearing the explanation. "I see. So humankind still has some strongholds left."

"We've told you our side of things. Could you share yours?" Elfiné asked.

"I've come here to strike down the goddess," Arle admitted after a pause, gripping the sword in her hands tightly.

"...Goddess?" Elfiné and Regina exchanged a look.

"...So the legend hasn't survived the years," Arle whispered to herself with a hint of disappointment upon seeing the bemused reactions. "I suppose it stands to reason. It has been one thousand years..."

Raising her voice, she then addressed Elfiné, Regina, and Sakuya.

"I have no duty to tell you. I, erm, I'm grateful for your poultice, but I implore you to leave me be."

"I'm sorry, but we can't do that." Elfiné shook her head. "You might be the sole survivor here. We can't abandon you. Part of a Holy Swordsman reconnaissance team's duty is to shelter refugees."

"..."

"We won't mistreat you, so how about staying with us for a while?" Sakuya retrieved something from a pocket and offered it to Arle.

"...What is this thing?" Arle asked.

"It's called a *monaka*. It's a treat I'm fond of."

"Y-you are trying to win me over with a treat?" Arle's face twisted in anger, and she bared her small teeth. "Do you take me for a child?!"

As if on cue, however, her stomach let out an adorable growl.

"..." The members of the eighteenth platoon remained silent.

"D-do as you'd like!" Arle looked away, her cheeks visibly flushed.

◆

What is that woman doing here?

As she watched over the group from the shadows of the ruins, Shary's hands froze in midair just as she was about to take a bite of a doughnut.

Arle Kirlesio, the Sword Tempest Fae. A princess of the Spirit Forest and final apprentice to Shardark, the Six Heroes' Swordmaster. Many generals of the Dark Lords' Armies had fallen to her blade. She was regarded as a one-woman battalion on the battlefield. She'd even infiltrated Necrozoa's Death Hold three times over and made attempts on Leonis's life.

I'd heard she went missing after the battle for the Skeleton Fort... Shary narrowed her crimson eyes. What was this swordswoman, who had menaced the Dark Lords' Armies, doing in this era? The elves were known for their longevity, but they weren't immortal. At best, they lived to be three hundred. Not even one of their kind could live for a thousand years.

Perhaps she was reborn as my lord was?

That couldn't be it. The reincarnation ritual was a thirteenth-order spell, accomplished only with assistance from the goddess Roselia. Even the elven sages would not have been able to achieve such a feat.

Either way, I must investigate this carefully.

It appeared Arle was injured, but Shary's master often warned her against acting recklessly. Swallowing a piece of her doughnut, Shary faded into shadow.

◆

Leonis's magical light cast a soft glow over the vast warehouse. As Riselia waited for her body to heal naturally, Leonis investigated the place.

"I found some food, Miss Selia," he called, carrying over a box of preserves. According to the expiration date on them, they were still safe for consumption.

They've been sitting here for ten years. Just what kind of marvels have humans developed? Leonis thought with incredulity. He could achieve a similar result using a time fixation spell, but that was eighth-order magic, far beyond what regular people could achieve.

"Hmm, so how is this supposed to be eaten...?" Leonis took out one of the pouches and read the instructions.

"Do you want me to make it for you, Leo?" Riselia inquired.

"Stop treating me like a child. I can handle this on my own."

"R-really? All right. I'll leave it to you, Leo." Riselia smiled, seemingly a bit happy.

Hmm. The instructions say to heat it with fire. Leonis lit a small flame over his fingertip and tried to warm the bag.

"...L-Leo! A pot! You're supposed to cook it with water in a pot!"

"A pot?"

"Yes. You boil the water and put it in."

"Understood."

Leonis summoned a metallic vessel from his vault in the Realm of Shadows. It was a priceless treasure called the Holy Grail. The Dark Lord had pillaged it from some country or another, but it would do fine for this purpose. Leonis poured some water he had stored and dumped the sealed pack's contents into the liquid.

"That's how it's done...right?"

"Yep, you did it. Good on you." Riselia patted Leonis on the head. As she did so, however, Leonis noticed that her cheeks were reddening. *Her breathing is a bit labored, too. Is something wrong with her?*

"You should rest a little, Miss Selia," instructed Leonis.

"Y-yeah…" She nodded with a slightly haggard voice.

As Leonis waited for the water to boil, he tried to put his thoughts into order. *First Archsage Arakael, and now she's back…*

Tearis Resurrectia was one of Leonis's sworn enemies, yet he had never fought her directly during his reign as the Undead King. Her powers could heal and revive, making them the opposite of Leonis's death-based ones.

She empowered the gods' armies and resurrected human warriors time after time as they perished on the battlefield. That was the Holy Woman's role within the Six Heroes.

I suppose that answers one question, though.

Tearis was a symbol to followers of the Holy Sect. The Voids she produced had likely been the ones that'd drawn the symbol Leonis had spotted around the Third Assault Garden.

The Holy Woman was consumed by the Voids, same as Arakael the Archsage. Why have the Six Heroes returned now, after all this time? Roselia never prophesized anything of the sort…

The mysterious invaders called Voids, humanity developing a society of oddly advanced magical technology, and the Holy Swords' peculiar power—none of it added up. It went beyond what the Goddess of Rebellion had foreseen.

"L-Leo…"

"?!"

Leonis stiffened as he realized Riselia's face was awfully close to his.

"M-Miss Selia?" Leonis swallowed nervously, feeling his heart skip a beat.

The silver-haired girl's cheeks were crimson. A faint breath escaped her lovely pink lips as her watery red eyes fixed themselves passionately on Leonis.

"I-I'm... I'm sorry, Leo..."

"...?"

"...I want your blood...," Riselia admitted in a coaxing whisper. Leonis could clearly hear her swallow.

Oh, right...

Riselia's healing ability consumed her mana, which spurred her vampiric impulse.

"U-understood," Leonis accepted, and he started rolling up one sleeve of his uniform. Before he'd finished, however...

"?!"

Riselia grabbed Leonis by the shoulders hard and thrust her small, newly formed fangs into his neck.

"Mmmm... Haaah... Nnng..."

"...M-Miss Selia... W-wait..."

"Mmm... *Schluuuurp*... Nha..."

Even when her thirst got the better of her, Riselia had always obeyed Leonis in the past. This time was very clearly different, however. She craved blood as if it was the only thing that mattered to her.

"W-Weoooo... I'm shorry..."

Riselia pushed Leonis down to the floor, nearly tearing his uniform off. This was the first time Leonis had ever seen Riselia behave this way. Perhaps the mixed emotions of returning to the ruins of her birthplace had left her unstable.

"Schlurp. Nibble. Nibble."

The curtain of Riselia's argent locks hung over his face.

"...A-aaah...!" A light moan escaped Leonis's throat.

Typically, Riselia's bloodsucking was accompanied by a sweet,

intoxicating pain. On this occasion, Leonis only felt a sharp stab into his neck, proof of how utterly lost to bloodlust Riselia was.

"Schlurp... Nibble. Nibble. Schlurp...!"

Leonis's magic flame flickered in the darkness as the suggestive sound of wet lips echoed through the warehouse.

"M-Miss...Selia..."

Boing. Riselia's soft, supple breasts pressed against Leonis's body. His fingertips reflexively grabbed tight at the back of the young woman's uniform.

"...Aah... Leo... Mmm, aah. ♪" Paying no mind to her disheveled skirt, Riselia continued biting into Leonis's neck. Her blouse came undone, slightly revealing the white underwear beneath.

"...Aah... W-we can't go...any further than this..." Leonis's fingers were gradually growing limp. Riselia had lost all reason and was now driven only by the vampiric urge.

Th-this is bad... Leonis's body was that of a ten-year-old. If this continued for much longer, Riselia would bleed him dry.

I have no choice... I have to use my sorcery to put her to sleep...

Leonis reached for the Staff of Sealed Sins lying on the ground, when...

"Mm... Weeeeo... Mha... *Schlrp...* Mm... ♪"

"—lia... Selia...!"

"Just...a little longer... Mm..."

"Erm... Selia, can you hear me?" A voice spoke to her from above.

"Ah... Mm... Haaaaaaa?!" At the sound of that voice, Riselia came to her senses and let out a panicked screech. "Elfiné?!"

Looking up, Leonis saw one of Elfiné's Eye of the Witch orbs floating nearby.

◆

"...I-I'm sorry we, erm, worried you, Miss Finé!" Riselia bowed apologetically in front of the sphere after fixing her clothes.

"...Your voice is kind of high-pitched. Is everything okay?"

"I-I-I'm perfectly fine! Peachy, even! You must be imagining it!" Riselia squeaked as she shook her head. Her face was practically a tomato.

"R-right..."

Thankfully, Riselia somehow managed to convince Elfiné nothing untoward was happening. Meanwhile, Leonis was languishing powerlessly on the floor behind Riselia's bowed figure.

I...really am...too soft when it comes to my minions..., Leonis chided himself as he listened in on Riselia and Elfiné's exchange. Back when he was the Undead King, he would never have allowed anyone to...manhandle him like that. A Dark Lord dying to a servant bleeding them out would undoubtedly become a shameful story mocked for centuries.

"I heard you two got into a tough scrap with some Voids. Are you injured?" Elfiné inquired.

"Y-yes. I'm a bit hurt, but it shouldn't get in the way of the mission."

"I'm surprised you're fine after falling from that height."

"Er, Leo used his Holy Sword's power...," Riselia managed evasively.

"Well, either way, I'm glad you're both all right. Regina and Sakuya are relieved, too."

Even though the only connection Riselia and Leonis had to the others was the orb, they still felt their comrades' sense of ease at knowing the pair was okay.

"You're at the bottommost underground sector right

now, right? We don't have a way to get down there, so we'll need to regroup somewhere on the surface."

"Roger. Ah, Miss Finé, there's something I have to report first," Riselia said.

"...Report?"

"Yes. There's a chance there's a Void Lord in this city."

"What?!" Elfiné cried in surprise.

Leaving out the part about the ghosts, Riselia told Elfiné about the Void they fought on the surface and that there was a chance that a Void Lord had merged with the mana furnace beneath the Central Garden.

The humans of this era did not believe in ghosts or other undead. Riselia correctly assumed that telling the others about the ghosts would simply confuse and distract them.

"A Void Lord... No...," Elfiné whispered in a strained voice.

"This is all speculation, of course, but...," Riselia began, now more composed, "since the Third Assault Garden is still advancing toward the Seventh, I think we should consider the possibility of a Stampede."

"You're right. If a gigantic Void appeared, it's likely a Void Lord was behind it. Either way, we have to investigate the mana furnace in the Central Garden." The Eye of the Witch orb flickered in midair, as if nodding.

"What about on your end, Elfiné? Anything happen?" Riselia asked.

"Erm..." Elfiné paused for a moment before replying. **"We... may have secured a civilian. An elf girl."**

"A civilian? You found a survivor in the ruins?!" Riselia exclaimed in surprise.

"No. She has a Holy Sword, so we're not sure if she's a civilian or not, but I think it'd be better if we tell you the details when we regroup."

"A-all right, understood. Where do we rendezvous, then?"

"Well, this is your hometown. Do you have somewhere in mind?"

Riselia paused for thought, then said, "How about the Crystalia estate at the Central Garden?"

"The Crystalia estate... Roger that. Regina can show us the way. Be careful, you two."

"Same to you all, too."

The transmission ended, and the Eye of the Witch sphere lost its light as it went into sleep mode. Evidently, keeping her Holy Sword active wore away at Elfiné's mental strength. Riselia took a deep breath and turned around to face Leonis.

"Finally feeling calmer?" Leonis asked with a hint of malice.

"...I-I'm sorry, Leo!" Riselia apologized, her face red.

"I told you you're allowed to drink some blood, but if you suck too much... It's, well, a problem."

"...U-um, that was, m-my mind went blank. I wasn't myself, and..." Riselia's shoulders slumped. There were tears in her eyes.

That's probably enough antagonizing.

Ever kind to his favorite minion, Leonis cleared his throat and said, "I was joking. I'm glad you've recovered your mana, Miss Selia."

"Leo..."

"Let me rest a while longer, and then we can head to the rendezvous point," Leonis said, rising to his feet. While anemic and dizzy, he could still move. Pouring some of the ration stew he'd heated up into a bowl, he handed it to Riselia.

"Thank you." Riselia brought her hands together in gratitude and smiled.

"By the way, that Crystalia estate you mentioned to Miss Elfiné..."

"Yeah. It's my family home," Riselia confirmed. "It's on the island at the heart of this city, the administrative ward in the Central Garden. Most buildings are destroyed beyond recognition, so we can't use them as landmarks, but I figured Regina and I could find the Crystalia estate easily enough. And..."

Riselia trailed off. Even without putting it into words, Leonis understood the reason. Her father, Duke Crystalia, could be wandering the remnants of his home, just as the souls of the Crystalia Knights had been down here.

Or perhaps he's already been turned into a Void by the Holy Woman...

Either way, Leonis was as interested in investigating the place as Riselia was. He had to uncover the truth of all this.

♦

On the lowermost underground level beneath the Central Garden, the mana furnace stood, emitting a glow that illuminated the walls around it.

"Aaah, soon. Soon, the goddess's vessel shall be filled."

In that quiet, templelike place, a young man in a priest's garb—Nefakess Void Lord—enjoyed a laugh. He stood before an altar where several dozen Demon Swords that his cult had gathered were resting. He took each one and thrust it into the mana furnace, as if adding fuel to a fire.

Vnnn... Vnnn... Vnnn...

Each sword Nefakess offered was swallowed up by the mana furnace.

"Oh, goddess, we've waited one thousand long years." Nefakess looked up, his eyes full of ecstasy. "The lofty one, the sole divinity brave enough to oppose the Luminous Powers..." His eyes were fixed on the pale form of the woman fused with the mana furnace.

The Holy Woman of the Six Heroes had reappeared in the same

era as a certain deity. Her lightless eyes gazed blankly into the air as her lips whispered a hymn.

"Aaah, such a sweet tone, Tearis Resurrectia. To think the song of the sworn enemy of my goddess's armies would ever be so pleasant to my ears."

The hero consumed by the Voids would now serve as the vessel of rebirth for the Goddess of Rebellion. A fragment of Roselia Ishtaris's soul would rise again within this emptiness.

"...Soon. It will come soon..."

Just as Nefakess finished throwing the last of the Demon Swords into the furnace, a dove-shaped Artificial Elemental landed on his shoulder.

"What? How boorish." He grimaced upon hearing its report, but his expression soon returned to its usual calm. "The angel was destroyed?" He'd dispatched that massive Void to dispose of the assassin from the Sanctuary.

Did I underestimate that elven hero? No...

Nefakess activated a terminal linking into the Assault Garden's security system. After a moment, the network detected a suspicious object nearby—an imperial combat aircraft.

"...A Holy Swordsmen investigation team. They found this place faster than I expected." Nefakess shrugged with a tired sigh. It was hard to believe mere Holy Swordsmen had defeated that angel. "Well, so be it. I suppose I should go and clean out the trash," Nefakess whispered, looking up at the pulsating mana furnace with a satisfied smile.

CHAPTER 7

THE CRYSTALIA ESTATE

"The subway tunnel leading to the Central Garden should be up ahead," Riselia said, pointing at the map displayed on her terminal.

It was a direct route passing right below the linking bridge to the Assault Garden's administrative ward.

"Can't we take the subway train?" Leonis asked.

"Leo, it's not the same as operating other vehicles," Riselia chided, holding up her index finger with a self-important smile.

Evidently, the Dark Lord had inquired about something strange.

"We'll walk along the rails by foot," Riselia decided. "It should save us some time compared to trekking across the surface."

"By foot...?" Leo asked, visibly fed up.

"Once we get back to Excalibur Academy, I'm going to add more stamina training to your curriculum," Riselia commented upon noticing his tone. "Okay, let's get moving."

"Ah, wait a moment." Leonis stopped Riselia before she set off.

"...Leo?"

"Miss Selia, there's something I want to give you."

"Something...for me?" Riselia cocked her head in surprise.

"Those ghost knights said the souls that were closer to the mana furnace turned into Voids more quickly," Leonis started.

"...Right."

"After what happened before, I'm not sure I'll always be able to safeguard you from harm..." Leonis looked down at Riselia's legs.

Her Vampire Queen powers had healed the broken limbs already, but one wrong step could have resulted in graver injuries.

"Are you worried about me, Leo?"

"I-I'm just saying you ought to be able to protect yourself, that is all." Leonis turned away from the young woman gazing intently at him.

Letting out a dry cough, the Dark Lord tapped the Staff of Sealed Sins's shaft against his shadow. A ripple spread through his ebon reflection, and from the center of those wrinkles, something appeared, shining with mystifying light.

It was a beautiful crimson dress the shade of the Underworld's blood flowers. It had a very striking design with a daring neck plunge. Its hems and cuffs were embroidered with threads infused with mana.

"...Clothing?" Riselia's ice-blue eyes widened.

"Yes. It's called the Bride's Dress."

"Huh? B-bride?!" Riselia's face turned a color that rivaled the outfit's. "L-Leo, erm... I'm really happy, but.... Wh-what do I do...?" She brought a hand to her mouth, confused.

"Wh-what are you assuming here?" Leonis said hurriedly. "This is an item of the highest grade, one I would only grant to a minion who serves as my right hand. I thought it was too soon to bequeath this to you, but given the situation, I believe I would present it to you now."

The gown was a hero-class item. Its proper name was the True Ancestor's Dress. It was one of the most precious things Leonis kept stored in his treasure vault in the Realm of Shadows. He'd stolen the outfit from a vampire castle he'd visited with Blackas.

Leonis had planned to wait until Riselia became more adept at controlling her mana, but this felt like an excellent chance to bequeath it to her.

"The True Ancestor's Dress will take a Vampire Queen's mana and use it to reinforce her body. Your strength will skyrocket, but it will also consume your mana rapidly. So do be discreet with its use," instructed Leonis. He held up his staff and chanted an incantation. The gown quickly folded up and sank into Riselia's shadow.

"It's gone?!"

"Merged into your shadow. When you want to call it, just imagine yourself wearing the dress and take in your mana. It shouldn't be too difficult."

"...U-understood." Riselia nodded gravely. "Thank you, Leo. I'll cherish it."

"There's no need for gratitude," Leonis replied, coughing dryly again. "A minion must always protect her master. While we're here, I'll have my elite knights escort you."

"Elite knights?"

"Yes. Come forth from the Realm of Shadows, the Three Champions of Rognas!" Leonis chanted, an indomitable smile on his lips.

A magic circle etched itself into the ground and then lit up with an ominous glow. And appearing at the center of that array were three skeleton warriors, each of them wielding a magical weapon.

"I am the Gelid Warrior, Amilas!" A skeleton wielding a sword and wearing leather armor struck a pose.

"I am Hell's Grappler, Dorug!" A heavily-armored skeleton holding an iron ball assumed another pose.

"And I am the Underworld's Archmage, Nefisgal!" Lastly, a robed skeleton holding a staff took a third pose.

""""And together, we are the illustrious Three Champions of Rognas!""""

The moment Riselia saw the three of them...

"..."

...Her expression visibly clouded over.

"More skellies...?" she asked.

"N-no, no! They're not like the skeletons you used for training!" Leonis corrected hurriedly.

They didn't look too different from the usual fare, so Riselia's reaction wasn't much of a surprise. However, not only were they stronger than any skeleton soldier, these three were elite combatants that surpassed even the Death Knights Leonis had summoned aboard the *Hyperion*.

"These are my comrades in arms. Seasoned warriors that accompanied me on the battlefield."

"...Th-they are?" Riselia blinked at the three skeletons dubiously. "They look, uh, kind of tangled."

"Nnng! Dorug, get away from me!"

"Mmm! No, Amilas, you get away from me!"

"Both of you, stay still! You're cracking my old bones!"

The concerning sound of snapping echoed through the underground passage.

What are these fools doing?! Leonis massaged his temples.

"Hold still," Riselia instructed as she carefully separated the trio's tangled bits. "Erm, it's like this... And like this..." Eventually, she separated the three skeletons from each other.

"Oooh! You have our thanks, beauteous princess!"

"We shan't forget this debt. We shall protect you with our lives!"

"The undead have no lives to give, though. Ka-ka-ka!"

Amilas, Dorug, and Nefisgal all rattled their skulls in laughter. Riselia turned a worried glance at Leonis that seemed to ask if the three were truly up to the task.

"Th-their skill is guaranteed!" Leonis said evasively.

"I am most honored to be able to serve a Vampire Queen, the noblest of undead!" Amilas exclaimed.

"Indeed, for only chaste virgins are said to be able to become Vampire Queens," Dorug needlessly appended.

"Vir—" Riselia blushed.

But then...

Bang!

Leonis beat Dorug, the grappler, over the head, sending his bones scattering over the ground.

"Mm, that hurt, Lord Leonis!" Dorug exclaimed without a hint of pain as his bones reassembled themselves.

"...B be quiet! Do not drag my name through the mud any longer!" Leonis brandished his staff in anger, throwing the three skeletons into Riselia's shadow.

◆

After walking for roughly fifteen minutes, Riselia and Leonis reached an abandoned terminal. There were several small rail cars lined up in an abandoned port.

"This looks good," Leonis said, tapping on the flank of a black-dyed one.

"That's a special carriage for royalty and nobles. I traveled in it a few times when I was little," Riselia said, rubbing the surface of the car nostalgically.

"Then how about we take it?"

"Huh?"

"Savel!" Leonis chanted before the silver-haired girl had time to react.

Whoosh! A blade of flames formed in front of Leonis and slashed the train car's coupling apart.

"Wait, Leo, what are you doi—?"

"Walking for hours is a bit too tiring, I think." Leonis pointed his staff at the ground and began to intone a bit of summoning magic. "Dead Carriers That Perished on the Battlefield, Rise Forth From the Realm of Shadows, Ye Steeds of War."

The darkness beneath Leonis rippled, and something crept out from within it.

"Sssss... Ssss...!" Crimson eyes shone eerily in the gloom. Two massive, skeletal war steeds appeared, their bodies wreathed in blue flames. These were fearsome horses that galloped across the battlefields—bone mares, high-level undead familiars employed by Leonis.

"Bony horses?" asked Riselia.

"They usually come with a war carriage." Leonis shrugged and shook his head.

His personal conveyance had large scythes attached to each wheel, but it had been destroyed in the last battle of the war, along with the Reaper who rode it, by the Six Heroes' Swordmaster, Shardark.

The two bone mares neighed loudly and walked ahead a few steps. The blue flames burning around their bodies wrapped around the train car.

"With this, the metal carriage can be towed by my bone mares," Leonis stated, tapping a door into the thing and chanting an unlocking spell.

The frame lit up and obediently swung open. Even these

advanced magical apparatuses functioned on the basic principles of sorcery. Simple ones could be easily operated, even by ancient spells.

"Let's get on, Miss Riselia," Leonis said, offering his hand. The young woman stood still in shock.

❖

"This thing looks like it can still move, Miss Elfiné. Any way we can get it to run?" Regina leaned forward, examining a military vehicle's wheels.

"It's got an authentication lock on it. I'll see what I can do," Elfiné replied, deploying the Eye of the Witch to try cracking the seal.

Arle watched the two of them, still gripping her sword. Her long ears would twitch now and then as she listened to the exchange. Elves perceived the voice of the wind and possessed far greater hearing than humans. Eavesdropping afforded Arle some information.

It looks like they really are here to investigate the city, she concluded silently.

These girls were apparently this era's equivalent of knights. They fought those distorted monsters. Their strange powers, which they called Holy Swords, operated differently than magic.

Compared with sorcery, it's significantly less versatile, but... Arle winced, holding her aching side. *If only one of them could use holy magic, they'd be able to heal me...* She increased her mana circulation to hasten her body's recovery, but the wound would still require time to heal.

I let the enemy get the better of me. So shameful...

Arle had never imagined that something as powerful as that large angel-like monster could exist. Of course, she was also aware that her skill with the blade was a far cry from what it had been in her heyday. Arle had spent a thousand years sleeping inside the Elder Tree, after all.

If I could at least fully regain my intuition... She held tight to Crozax's hilt. More than anything, Arle wanted to know who that man who had summoned the abomination was.

A guardian of the goddess's vessel?

The Elder Tree, who had given Arle her mission, had considered the possibility that the Goddess of Rebellion might have a guardian. Some adherent of Roselia Ishtaris, perhaps, who would wish to see her resurrection come to fruition.

The missing Dark Lords were likely candidates for such a role. For example, the so-called Undead King, Leonis Death Magnus. He was known for being more powerful than his peers. When all the other Dark Lords had fallen, he alone had continued the fight.

It was said the Undead King left behind a foreboding prophecy before Necrozoa's fall: "So long as darkness exists in this world, I shall rise again and again to cast everything into terror."

Leonis was a ruler who had overcome death. If any of the Dark Lords had managed to be resurrected, it was likely him.

Or perhaps Azra-Ael, the Devil of the Underworld?

However, there was another Dark Lord who hadn't been confirmed as deceased. Azra-Ael had been sealed in the throne room of his Otherworldly Castle by the Archsage Arakael Degradios. Of the Eight Dark Lords, Azra-Ael and Leonis had been the most loyal to the Goddess of Rebellion.

Was that man a lackey of the Dark Lords, or does he serve someone else...? Arle pondered, her gaze cast on the ground.

"Does it still hurt?" the blue-haired girl squatted down and asked.

If Arle recalled correctly, her name was Sakuya. She had a cool-looking expression and beautiful features.

"...Yes," Arle replied curtly and looked up. This one had been designated as her guard.

"I'm sorry. If we had a medical expert, we might have been able to help more," Sakuya said, eyeing Arle's bloodstained bandages.

"It's not a serious wound. It'll heal soon enough," Arle replied, though she averted her gaze.

Sakuya took a seat next to Arle and looked her over. "That's a fine weapon. Does it have a name?" she asked, her eyes falling to Crozax, cradled in Arle's arms.

"The Demon Smiting Sword."

"That's quite the grand title," Sakuya remarked, her curiosity growing.

"Yes...," Arle said curtly, and then she asked, "Why did you stop your blade when we fought?"

"I just did, I suppose. Crossing swords with you made me realize that you weren't a bad person."

"...What does that mean? Do you possess some kind of insight ability?"

"Something like that. My intuition is usually right." The blue-haired girl smiled sardonically.

"You're strong," Arle stated. "Not as strong as me, though."

"Am I?"

"What country's sword style did you use?" Arle asked, her curiosity piqued.

Sakuya fell silent for a moment before answering, "The Sakura Orchid. It was a style passed down in my family called the Ultimate Blade Technique. My older sister and I were its only successors."

"I've never heard of such a place."

A country by that name hadn't existed in Arle's native era.

"Hardly matters. It no longer exists," Sakuya admitted quietly. "My home was destroyed by the Voids."

"...I see. Forgive my tactless question." Arle hung her head, coiling her ponytail around a finger. "My nation is gone as well."

Sakuya's blue eyes widened in surprise.

"It was in a forest. The sanctuary of the elves and the spirits. A silent, beautiful place."

"...Was it the Voids?"

"No." Arle shook her head. "Dizolf Zoa, the Lord of Rage... I suppose that name means nothing to you, though."

Dizolf Zoa had reigned over the Saag mountain range and was the cruelest of the Eight Dark Lords. The armies of ogres he unleashed on the forest trampled and destroyed everything.

I won't let that happen ever again, thought Arle as she looked down at her sword. The weapon's sole purpose was to destroy the source of all calamities—the goddess Roselia Ishtaris.

"Ah, looks like that's got it working." The blond girl waved over Arle and Sakuya. Apparently, they'd managed to get the vehicle running.

"...Where are we going?" Arle asked.

"The city's administrative ward, the Central Garden. We'll regroup with our comrades there."

"So it's not just you three here?"

"That's right." Sakuya nodded and showed Arle a small device.

Projected on its screen was the image of a girl with silver hair. Even by elven standards, she was beautiful. Next to her picture was that of...

"...A child?"

It was a boy with fair features.

"Yes, this is Leonis. A ten-year-old boy we found in different ruins a while back," Sakuya explained. "His power as a Holy Swordsman is vast, though."

Even a boy of such tender years has to fight against these terrible monsters? The situation must truly be dire. But that aside...

"Leonis?" Arle furrowed her brow. "What an inauspicious name for one to bear."

"...?"

"That name is greatly hated in my homeland—"

A shrill roar interrupted Arle. The vehicle was ready to go.

"Great job, Elfiné. You broke through military authentication like it was nothing," praised the blond.

"It's easy compared to the capital's security. Regina, can you show us the way?"

"Yeah, leave it to me. Sakuya, let's go."

"All right." Sakuya got to her feet and extended a hand to Arle. "Can you stand?"

"...I'll be fine on my own," the half-elf insisted. She rose and picked up Crozax.

◆

Trtrtrtrtrtrtr!

The metallic rails spat sparks as the sound of horseshoes clicking against the ground echoed. The improvised bone train blitzed through the underground tunnel, leaving a cacophonous rumble in its wake. Altogether, the sounds became a terrible roar that seemed to herald the end of the world. The bone mares' crimson eyes illuminated the darkness like searchlights.

Sitting inside the train car's furnished interior, Leonis composedly sipped from a can of coffee. It was standard canned coffee sold in Excalibur Academy's school store.

"It's a bit loud, but otherwise quite convenient."

"Yeah..." Riselia, who sat opposite Leonis, gazed at him fixedly.

"What's wrong, Miss Selia?" Leonis asked, furrowing his brow.

"Ah, erm... Sorry." The young woman waved her hands apologetically.

"If it's the speed, going any faster risks derailing the carriage..."

"No, that's not it. I just thought that you're..." Riselia paused, as if carefully choosing her words. "You're kind of like...a Dark Lord."

"...?! Pfha, pfft!" Leonis gagged on his coffee.

"Ahhh! Are you all right, Leo?!" Riselia hurried over, taking out a handkerchief to wipe his trousers clean.

"...Wh-what did you just say...?" Leonis asked between coughs.

True, he had shown Riselia a bit of his Dark Lord power, but he hadn't revealed the true nature of his identity. Riselia should have still believed Leonis to be an ancient sorcerer who'd lost his memory.

"It's a fairy tale my father told me when I was still little," Riselia explained, folding up her handkerchief. "Looking at you reminded me of the Dark Lord from that story."

"A fairy tale...?" Leonis patted his chest, feeling no small sense of relief. She hadn't discovered his secret.

"A Dark Lord riding on a skeletal horse lives in a castle of bones with his many retainers. He could make lightning fall from the sky and breathe fire."

"Fire breathing?! That's absurd!" Leonis refuted despite himself.

"R-really? But Father said the Dark Lord could breathe fire...," Riselia stated, cocking her head quizzically.

Hmm...

Riselia's story didn't seem more than a harmless children's tale, but it was amusing in its own way. As far as Leonis had researched, much of his era's knowledge had not survived to the present day. However, there was a chance that legends of gods and Dark Lords remained in folktales.

"Oh, but when I said you remind me of that Dark Lord, I didn't mean it in a bad way."

"...There's a good meaning to 'Dark Lord'?" Leonis questioned, slightly astonished.

"Father would always tell me that a scary Dark Lord would come to defeat the Voids."

"..."

Silence hung over the carriage, save the sound of the bone mares' hooves. Said Dark Lord was indeed sitting right in front of Riselia. Yet, it hardly meant anything. Leonis was confident that the story about the frightening savior was just a kind lie a father had told to soothe his daughter.

"I'm sorry. That was a strange thing to say," Riselia admitted while peering out the window. "I just thought, 'What if that scary Dark Lord really did appear?'"

"No, I'm honored. A mere sorcerer like me being called a Dark Lord," Leonis replied with a composed smile. "By the way, what becomes of the Dark Lord in that story?"

"The same thing that always happens. A hero defeats the Dark Lord, and everyone lives happily ever after."

"...What a sorry excuse for a fairy tale."

"Huh?"

"Never mind."

◆

"Hiiiiiiiiiiii!"

The bone mares let out a loud neigh that echoed through the tunnel, fitting their name's resemblance to the word *nightmare*.

"It seems we've arrived."

Leonis tapped his staff on the floor, and the car gradually decelerated before coming to a complete stop. The door opened, and Leonis and Riselia disembarked at the terminal. Part of the carriage was jutting out of the station, but Leonis shrugged it off as being within an acceptable margin of error.

The bony horses that towed the train car exhausted their mana and fell apart. Leonis's shadow swelled up and swallowed their scattered remains. He'd considered taking the car along with them, but...

"The Realm of Shadows' vault is already filled to the brim!"

...Thinking back to Shary's angry chiding, Leonis decided against it.

"How does your shadow keep doing that?" Riselia asked, cocking her head. She gingerly stepped over Leonis's dark reflection—nothing happened.

"I think you're better off not knowing what goes on in there," Leonis replied with an indomitable smile.

Riselia couldn't imagine that it contained the entirety of the Realm of Shadows. And in truth, even Leonis wasn't sure of all that occurred in the depths of that place. The graveyard located in the deepest recesses of the realm was where his strongest minion was sealed, but Leonis had no plans of awakening it for the time being. That one was beyond Leonis's ability to control, at least for now.

As the pair advanced through the dark underground, they discovered an elevator that led up to the surface.

"This one isn't usable, right?" Leonis asked.

"Yeah. Let's take the stairs," Riselia answered.

"...Yes, I assumed as much." Leonis sighed, making his disgruntlement known.

Climbing so many steps was hard on the untrained body of a ten-year-old.

"Think of it as stamina training, all right?" Riselia said, patting Leonis on the head as she set off cautiously.

Only the sound of their footfalls filled the silence. Leonis ascended the staircase with Riselia leading him by the hand.

Wouldn't blowing off the ceiling and using a flying spell speed this up? Leonis wondered as he struggled for breath.

"This kind of reminds me of when I first found you," Riselia suddenly whispered during their climb.

"...Yes, it does," Leonis agreed.

Back then, Riselia had held his hand as they'd departed the Grand Mausoleum. Shortly after, Voids had attacked, and Riselia had sacrificed herself to protect Leonis.

At the time, I only saw her as a source of information, Leonis recalled with a bittersweet smile.

"...Back then, the door opened on its own, and I was able to save you, Leo."

"A door?"

"Yeah, the one to the room you were trapped in. It had ancient letters etched on it, and while I was trying to decipher them, it just..."

"...Oh, yes. Right."

That was something Leonis was curious about, as well. The door to the underground crypt that housed the Undead King's casket was heavily sealed to keep everyone out. For one thousand years, that deterrent served its purpose perfectly. So then, how had Riselia managed to break it so effortlessly?

I doubt it was due to some flaw in the spell...

"We should reach the surface soon," Riselia encouraged.

And after five more minutes of tiringly pushing up steps, they finally reached the surface. The pair were now in the Central Garden train station of the Third Assault Garden's administrative ward.

"The estate should only be a short distance from here," remarked Riselia.

"M-more walking?" Leonis whined, clearly fed up.

"Just a little longer." Riselia smiled softly and ruffled Leonis's hair.

◆

The gate to the Crystalia home was broken, and the garden inside was in a sorry state. At this point, calling it such was wrong. The miasma had caused all the flora to shrivel up and die, leaving only a devastated wasteland.

Riselia entered the premises, the gravel crackling under her feet.

A homecoming for the first time in six years, eh? Leonis followed the silver-haired girl wordlessly. Usually, she matched Leonis's pace when she walked, but this time she didn't have the presence of mind to do so. Beyond the ruined garden was a large building that was evidently the mansion itself.

It reminded Leonis of the Hræsvelgr dorm, in the sense that it was designed after the architectural style of the old kingdom of Londirk. It was likely what passed for retro-culture in the eyes of this era's nobility. It certainly stood out when compared to the laminated buildings that surrounded it.

Walking along the paved road leading up to the mansion, they reached the front door.

"It doesn't look like the lock is operating," Riselia observed, and then she nodded once. "Hyaaahhh!" She filled her fist with mana and punched through the reinforced door, reducing it to splinters.

"That's barbaric, Miss Selia," Leonis chided her.

Riselia hurried inside, not paying Leonis's words any mind. Thick layers of accumulated dust danced through the air, making her cough a little. Past the entry was a lobby. There were staircases on both sides, leading up to the second story.

"This place seems comparatively untouched," Leonis observed, conjuring an orb of light at the tip of his staff.

"Yeah. We'd evacuated the estate by the time the Voids got here."

The abode seemed almost oppressively quiet. The only reprieve was the sound of Leonis and Riselia's footsteps.

No sign of any ghosts here.

According to the Crystalia Knights' ghosts, the dead souls that wandered along the Central Garden had all been turned into humanoid Voids.

"I'll check the inside of the mansion. Want to come with me?" Riselia asked.

"It's better if I remain outside. Regina and the others might show up," replied Leonis. He wasn't that gauche. Riselia would undoubtedly want to be alone at a time like this.

After igniting a light on a portable device she'd brought with her, Riselia ascended to the estate's second floor.

◆

The door to the study swung open, its hinges letting out a shrill creak. Taking a deep breath, Riselia stood in the doorway for a moment. The room wasn't large. Its walls were lined with shelves stocked full of ancient magical apparatuses and texts excavated from ruins. Six years had done little to alter this chamber. It was as if time stood still here.

When she was little, Riselia would often sneak here to read. Thinking back on it, she realized that perhaps her interest in investigating ancient ruins had been fostered by her father.

And thanks to that, I saved Leo from that underground crypt.

Trodding on layers of dust, Riselia moved past the entryway and into the study. Inside were a large work desk and a chair. She strained her eyes, but of course, Duke Edward's ghost was nowhere to be seen.

Was her father's soul still wandering this city? Or was he…?

Riselia shook her head to banish that terrible thought from her mind. She then noticed a tome sitting on the desk. It had a leather binding but no title.

"…A book? What is this? Ancient writing?"

Sweeping the dust off the old text, she started leafing through the pages.

I've never seen this language before…

Riselia's primary focus of study at Excalibur Academy was old cultures and ruins investigation. She was one of the more knowledgeable students when it came to ancient languages. However, whatever was written in this book, it used a system that was unlike anything Riselia had seen before. It seemed wholly alien.

The last book Father researched…

With her interest piqued, Riselia picked up the volume.

This is a memento...

Leaving the study, she headed for her old bedroom. That was when...

"I was wondering who trespassed on this city, but aren't you the lovely little lady?"

"...Who are you?!" Riselia wheeled around, sensing a presence from behind her.

It was a slender young man with peculiar facial features. He wore an anachronistic white robe and looked to be in his twenties. He had a pleasant smile on his lips, but something about it filled Riselia with an eerie sense of dread.

Filled with an instinctive sense of danger, Riselia jumped away at once.

"Holy Sword, Activate!"

The Bloody Sword manifested in Riselia's right hand. The young man watched her with interest in his eyes.

"So you're a Holy Swordswoman, after all. I'd hoped to carry on in secret, but I suppose humanity's technology has advanced to the point where we're beyond caring for appearances."

"...Who are you?" Riselia demanded again. "What is a human doing here?"

"...Human? Oh, you mean me?" The young man flashed Riselia a gruesome smile. *"I daresay that's the biggest insult I've ever heard."*

"...?!"

"You'll find I'm not as magnanimous as those who command me. The debt of your insult shall be collected in blood."

The man dressed as a priest held up his hand, and a helix of crimson flames burst from his fingers.

"Farga!"

◆

Leonis went out to the estate's courtyard and took a seat on one of the garden rocks, polishing a dragon's bone. It was one of his hobbies. Well-polished bones added to a skeleton's dignity when put into use. As the Undead King, Leonis regularly made use of skeletons.

It wouldn't do for my enemies to mistake my soldiers for those used by the average necromancer or lich.

This was something of an obsession of Leonis's. Further complicating things was that bones were seemingly harder to come by in this era. Leonis was unsure whether dragons even existed in this day at all.

I might have tens of thousands of troops slumbering in the Realm of Shadows, but I should be frugal…

"…id… **Can you hear me, kid?**" The Eye of the Witch sitting next to Leonis lit up, emitting a crackling voice.

"Miss Regina?" Leonis replied, his hands stopping.

"**Ah, great. Where are you right now?**"

"We're at the Crystalia estate."

"**Huh? How did you get there so quickly?**" Regina raised her voice in surprise.

"We used the underground railroad network to get directly to the Central Garden."

"**I mean, yeah, but the underground linear rail can't move, right?**"

"We got it to move," Leonis answered curtly, not feeling inclined to explain further. "Enough about that, though. Where are you?"

"**We're just heading for the linking bridge.**"

"I see. We'll wait for you here." Given how the Third Assault

Garden was broken up, Regina, Elfiné, and Sakuya would arrive within the hour.

"Yeah, please. By the way, where's Lady Selia?"

"In the mansion. I assumed I should give her some time for herself."

"That's pretty mature of you, kid." Leonis got the feeling Regina was smiling on the other side of the call. **"Ah, do you want to see my room? I'll let you in once we get there."**

"Oh, not really..."

"...D-don't you want to see a girl's room, kid?"

"Erm..."

But just as Leonis was about to answer...

Booooooooooooooooooooooooooooom!

Every window on the second story of the mansion burst out with a rumbling blast.

◆

A roaring explosion echoed as crimson flames consumed the corridors, reducing everything they touched to ashes.

"I may have overdone it against a mere human. A third-order spell is capable of killing a giant." Nefakess smiled, not a speck of soot on his robe. "Now then, how many more uninvited gnats must I sweep away...?"

The man turned to leave, waving his hand to ward off the smoke, when...

"...Hmm?"

He stopped in place. His brow furrowed with suspicion. There, between the cinders flitting through the air, was a robed skeleton.

"...What...?"

"Hmm, this is quite taxing on my old bones," the bony figure admitted, sticking out his staff and forming a glowing, blue magical barrier.

Pho Rias, the magic barrier spell, was fourth-order defensive sorcery, only usable by high-ranking sorcerers.

"...A skeleton?"

"Ka-ka-ka!" The undead thing gave an eerie, rattling cackle. "Don't lump me in with other gutless skeletons, whelp! For I am a high-ranking undead! An Elder Lich!"

"What...?!" Nefakess whispered.

The robed skeleton waved his staff, which lit up and produced dozens of mana arrows.

"...It can't be!" Nefakess exclaimed as he quickly chanted a defensive spell and blocked the conjured projectiles. "Why are there undead here...?!"

"Hmph, insolent fool. To make an attempt on our mistress's life!" a new skeleton, this one wielding a sword, declared.

"Just who is behind this...?!" Nefakess demanded. No sooner had he done so than a third warrior made of bones attacked from behind. This one was a hulking brute carrying an iron ball.

"...?!"

"I am the Gelid Warrior, Amilas!"

"I am Hell's Grappler, Dorug!"

"And I am the Underworld's Archmage, Nefisgal!"

The three champions stepped forward as one.

""""And together, we are the illustrious Three Champions of Rognas!"""" they cried in unison, each striking a unique pose.

"Wh-what's going on...?!" Nefakess's eyes darted about in confusion. "What are these creatures doing here...? How...?!"

The way they carried themselves was unquestionably absurd, but they were far stronger than ordinary undead. Nefakess could tell these were all seasoned warriors that rivaled heroes. Behind those three skeletons, a shadow rose to its feet. Its silvery locks wavered in the surging fire. Nefakess had thought he'd obliterated the Holy Swordswoman with his spell, but he couldn't have been more wrong.

"...Thank you, you three. You saved me," she said.

"Do not mention it, milady!" the archmage Nefisgal replied with a flourish of one hand. "You are dear to our lord's heart, after all! Now then, mistress, do you know who this ruffian might be?"

"...I have no idea." Riselia shook her head, her eyes fixed on Nefakess.

"Hmm. But he does look skilled," the warrior Amilas remarked. "It is best you retreat, my lady."

"No, I'm afraid I can't let you do that," Nefakess declared. "I thought you were nothing but an insignificant worm, but a human who commands such high-ranking undead is rare. You've piqued my interest, I'll admit. Just who are you?"

All at once, Nefakess's demeanor had changed. He pointed a finger at Riselia and began chanting. The air crackled at his words.

"This is a sixth-order spell—sorcery that's more powerful than anything a mere human could ever achieve." Nefakess's handsome lips curled up in cruel mocking. "Can you block this?"

"Get behind me, fair princess...!" Dorug, the grappler, called before leaping forward.

At the same moment...

"Miss Selia!"

"...!"

A boy's shout filled the room, and a fire spell lanced forth from behind Riselia. The magic flames quickly consumed Nefakess.

"...Leo?!" Riselia spun around to see Leonis with his Staff of Sealed Sins in hand.

◆

"L-Leo...," Riselia said, her ice-blue eyes wide with shock.

The boy was standing at the end of the corridor. "You're all right..." He sighed in relief.

The Three Champions of Rognas had kept Riselia safe.

"What happened? Who was that...?" Leonis asked.

"I don't know..." Riselia shook her head.

Leonis peered down the burning hallway. He'd fired a third-order explosive spell, magic that should have been enough to reduce any ordinary person to ash.

How untoward. I neglected to restrain myself, Leonis chided. When it came to this minion of his, the Dark Lord tended to lose his cool.

"Kch-heh-heh-heh..." Laughter could be heard from within the blaze.

"...?!"

"So you've brought someone else with you. That spell just now packed a bit of a punch. I'll grant you that."

A figure rose in the swaying flames. A young man clad in a priest's garb stepped out of the fire, brushing soot off his shoulders while wearing a composed grin. Leonis's eyes went wide with disbelief.

What?! How can it be? Why is he here?!

The man didn't regard Leonis's reaction with much interest, however.

"Ah-ha-ha, surprised? Yes, I suppose that sort of magic would have been enough to kill most." Nefakess extended his arm to gesture at the surrounding conflagration, misinterpreting Leonis's shock. "I'm sorry to disappoint, but an attack of that magnitude cannot kill me."

He chanted another spell, forming a ball of intense flame in his fingers.

Sorcery. I knew it. It really is him...

Just as Leonis was about to tell Nefakess to wait...

Voom!

The floor they were standing on started shaking on its own.

"What?" "Huh?!" Leonis and Riselia exclaimed at once.

Vrrrrrr! The trembling grew stronger. The tremors were so intense they rocked the manor's very foundation, causing Leonis to lose his footing and stumble.

"Wh-what is this?!" "'Tis a cataclysm!" "Protect the mistress!" the skeleton warriors shouted in panic.

An earthquake? It can't be. We're on the ocean.

Was it that man's doing? Leonis placed a hand on the wall to steady himself and looked up.

"Heh-heh-heh... Heh-heh... Ah-ha-ha-ha-ha, ha-ha-ha!" The man was laughing. He spread both hands as his face contorted with joy.

"...What's so funny?" Leonis asked suspiciously.

The question brought the man's ecstatic guffawing to an eerily swift halt. "She has awakened. Of course I would rejoice."

"...She?"

"Yes, the great goddess has awakened from the Holy Woman's vessel!" The priest turned his eyes toward the heavens, his expression still frozen in manic excitement.

"...*Goddess?* Did you just say *goddess*?" Leonis took a step forward, demanding an answer.

Crack...!

Before he could get any reply, however, a fissure ran across the man's face.

Crack... Crack... Crack...!

What?

The fractures expanded across his body, as if...

"...Hmm, I suppose the time is right. Fine, then," the mysterious person in priest attire remarked calmly, even as his body was splitting apart. "I admit I'm a bit disappointed that I won't be fortunate enough to see the goddess's resurrection with my own two eyes, but that is simply how things go. My job here is complete..."

Crack... Crack... Craaaaaaaaaaack...!

Breaks ran all over the young man's body, and the emptiness between them quickly overtook him.

"...Wait!"

"Stay where you are!"

Leonis and Riselia both broke into a run to catch the man, but...

"You shall serve as the first sacrifices offered up to the goddess."

By the time the pair reached him, his form had vanished, leaving only emptiness in its wake. The priest's disappearance hadn't brought an end to the quaking, however.

"Just who was he...? What goddess...?" Riselia was at a complete loss.

"...I don't know." Leonis shook his head. Internally, his mind was racing with contradictory thoughts and doubts.

What's going on here? Leonis had recognized that slender man in white robes. *There's no mistaking it. That was...*

Nefakess Reizaad. A confidant of Azra-Ael, the Devil of the Underworld, one of the Goddess of the Rebellion's most loyal servants.

I saw him a few times at the Gatherings of the Eight Dark Lords. He always shadowed Azra-Ael, not once setting foot on the battlefield. It looks like he didn't recognize me in my present form, but...

Why would a Dark Lord's confidant be at a place like this, in this age...?

And he definitely said "goddess." Leonis fell deep into contemplation.

"Leo, look at that!" Riselia pointed out the window.

A gigantic shape was beginning to rise from the Central Garden's heart.

CHAPTER 8

THE FALLEN GOD'S GLORY

A snarling rumble shook the Third Assault Garden. A clarion song rang through the gloom, cutting through the dark, stormy clouds above the ruined city. A beautiful voice was reciting a hymn of the Holy Sect.

In the depths of the Central Garden, at the bottom floor of the Third Assault Garden's military ward, from the place that could be called the very heart of this anti-Void fortress, something rose to the surface.

It tore through countless bulkheads, resounding as it slowly surfaced, dragging a large number of cables with it. Even the anti-Void weapons in its way were smashed aside all too easily. The mere peak of that monster's form breaching the ground caused the surrounding area to sink in. Buildings toppled one after another.

"...Is that the Void Lord...?!" Riselia ran out of the mansion but still couldn't believe her eyes.

A massive construct of stone and metal, made out of the Third Assault Garden's structures, erupted forth, standing tall as if to lord over the artificial island. It towered hundreds of meters in height, like a cathedral of old. At the top of that titanic construct was a glowing crystal-like formation.

Half-submerged into that stone was a pale-skinned woman.

"The Holy Woman, Tearis Resurrectia." Leonis whispered the name of his sworn enemy. She was one of the Six Heroes who had been granted the power to continually grow and evolve by the Luminous Powers. It was by way of that miraculous ability that Tearis had merged with the mana furnace.

No, that's not accurate... She's merged with the Third Assault Garden itself.

When the Archsage Arakael Degradios appeared in the Seventh Assault Garden, he'd attempted to merge with its mana furnace, as well. What Leonis saw now may well have been what the Archsage had tried to achieve.

"It took in the mana furnace!" Riselia exclaimed.

"Yes. It looks like those ghosts were telling the truth." Leonis looked up at the Void Lord, that man's words still clinging to his mind.

Nefakess Reizaad... He mentioned a goddess. That seemed to be how he'd described the Void Lord—a deity. While the creature certainly was imposing, something felt off about the conclusion to Leonis. *No. That might be the Holy Woman, but it's not the Goddess of Rebellion.* Leonis shook his head in denial.

Most important of all, as one of the Six Heroes, the Holy Woman, Tearis, was the sworn enemy of the Dark Lords' Armies. Even if Azra-Ael's aide was mistaken, he would never regard one of the Six Heroes as the Goddess of Rebellion. There had been many divine beings in the past, but there was only one the Dark Lords honored. And that was the one being who had opposed the Luminous Powers: the Goddess of Rebellion, Roselia Ishtaris.

What's going on here? Why did he call this monstrosity a goddess...?!

The Void Lord's song echoed through the gray sky, like a hymn meant to bless, or perhaps condemn, the world. Suddenly, the mana furnace began to emit an almost blindingly brilliant glow.

"Wh-what's going o—?"

As if to answer Riselia's question, the mana furnace shot a shaft of light into the sky.

Vrrrrrrrrrrrrrrrrrrrrrrrrrrrrrrrrr!

The bolt blew away the clouds that had blotted out the sun, revealing the boundless azure expanse above. The vibrations in the air reached the place Leonis was standing, making pebbles bounce off the ground.

Sunlight poured down from above, as though to bless the Void Lord's arrival.

"It...can't be..." Riselia swallowed nervously, her expression cramped with shock.

Had that blast been loosed at the ground, it would have wiped entire sectors of the Assault Garden away.

"If this thing reaches the Seventh..."

Excalibur Academy was home to many Holy Swordsmen, but would any number of them be enough to oppose this thing?

"...We have to stop it." Riselia clenched her fists, resolute.

"Wait, just wait." Leonis grabbed the young woman's arm before she ran off impulsively. "Are you trying to get yourself killed?"

"But if we don't stop it, everyone will... It'll happen again..."

Undoubtedly, this was calling up Riselia's terrible memories of the tragic Stampede from six years ago. The poor girl was trembling.

"I'll go fight it," Leonis declared.

"Leo?"

"Miss Riselia, wait here for Regina and the others. Regroup with them."

Leonis looked up, fixing his gaze on the Void Lord merged with the mana furnace. While his reasons were different, he couldn't let the thing do as it pleased, either. Tearis Resurrectia was a sworn enemy of Leonis's and placed his kingdom in danger, just as the Archsage Arakael had.

What's more, he still wanted to know why Nefakess had referred to her as a goddess.

"Amilas, Dorug, Nefisgal, keep her here," Leonis commanded as he turned his gaze to the three skeletons behind Riselia.

"""By your will!""" the bony heroes answered in chorus, and they sank into Riselia's shadow.

"Leo, let me come with you!"

"No, it's dangerous. Forget it." Leonis shook his head.

Riselia had undoubtedly grown quite strong, and the day when she'd be able to lead Leonis's undead legions as a full-fledged Vampire Queen was fast approaching. However, Leonis couldn't ignore the fact that she was still inexperienced.

"Leo…" Riselia squatted down and looked the boy straight in the eyes. Leonis felt his heart skip a beat.

"Six years ago, I couldn't do anything," she began, and Leonis noticed a faint wavering in her voice. "Father and the other Crystalia Knights… They all laid down their lives for me. All I could do was sit in the shelter, praying for the Dark Lord from the fairy tale to save me." Riselia bit her lip and continued with a hushed voice. "I don't want to feel that way ever again. I can't let you go alone, Leo."

Riselia wrapped Leonis's head in her arms and hugged him close.

"Miss…Selia…"

With his head cuddled like a child's, Leonis could only concede. Riselia's mind was made up. Nothing Leonis said would deter her.

She's bright, but stubborn. Though I suppose that's part of her merit. Leonis broke into a bitter smile. If Blackas heard of this, he'd comment that Lord Magnus was being too lenient with his minions.

"Very well. Come with me."

"...Leo!"

"But just this once." Leonis sighed.

Either way, so long as the Void Lord was out there, no place in this ruined city was truly safe. To that end, Riselia was probably better off at Leonis's side. The two watched as the gigantic thing slowly began to move.

"Let's hurry. There should be a two-seater vehicle behind the mansion."

◆

A military vehicle ran over the damaged wreckage of the road. And sitting in its carrying tray...

"...What's what?!" Regina shouted, the wind whipping her blond pigtails around. The Central Garden was ahead, linked to the rest of the city by a bridge. She pointed at the peculiar structure that was floating above it.

"That's the Void Lord," Elfiné said nervously, gripping the steering wheel in the front seat. An orb floated above her, busily processing information. "It's on the same level as the Void Lord who attacked the Seventh Assault Garden... No, it might even be stronger," she concluded.

"...A Void Lord, eh?" Sakuya whispered, her expression dark.

"Then Lady Selia's report..." Regina trailed off.

"Yes, it was accurate," answered Elfiné.

The vehicle ran over a bump, its tires jolting hard.

"This goes beyond the scope of an investigation," Elfiné

commented, glaring at the gigantic structure in the sky. "We have to retreat immediately and report this to the academy."

"But Lady Selia and the kid are still in the Central Garden," Regina tried to argue.

"I know that," Elfiné interjected, biting her lip as her fingers tightened around the steering wheel.

In this situation, the safe course of action would be to abide by the anti-Void combat manual and pull out. However, Elfiné had already lost two comrades once in what should have been a simple investigation mission. That was when her Holy Sword, the Eye of the Witch, had lost its original power.

I won't let that happen, not ever again! Elfiné stomped down on the accelerator pedal. With that massive monster in the sky, leaving the Third Assault Garden via the tactical fighter wasn't much of an option anyhow.

What do we do...?

Sitting inside the shaking carrying tray, Arle Kirlesio glared up at the Void Lord. "Roselia Ishtaris. To think she would resurrect using one of the Six Heroes as a vessel...!"

◆

"Hang on tight, Leo!"

"O-okay!" Leonis replied, wrapping his arms around Riselia's waist as hard as he could.

Her silvery hair trailed in the breeze, brushing against Leonis's cheek. The two-wheeled vehicle's magical motor roared to life. It took off, scattering rubble in its wake as it sped. Gritting his teeth to keep from biting his tongue, Leonis clung to Riselia's back.

He squinted against the wind that beat incessantly against his eyes. The Void Lord was moving, gliding through the air.

"We won't catch up to it at this rate... It's a bit dangerous, but we'll have to take the highway!" Riselia turned onto a wider road, which was thankfully still mostly intact. Leonis held on to her waist tightly to not be thrown off.

I—I have no choice but to do this! Leonis told himself as he felt his cheeks redden at the soft warmth of a girl's body.

Unfortunately, the pleasant moment was short-lived.

Crack! Crack! Crack!

"...?!"

Numerous fractures formed in the air around them.

"Voids?! Leo, be careful!"

Crack... Crack... Crack... Crack...!

More and more of the fissures carved their way into reality until they entirely obscured the way ahead. An army of humanoid Voids, the same ones Riselia and Leonis had encountered on the school rooftop, emerged from the rifts.

"The Crystalia Knights' ghosts...," Leonis heard Riselia whisper sorrowfully despite the air rushing in his ears.

This was all that remained of those brave, proud warriors who had fought to protect the Third Assault Garden to the very end. The Holy Woman had resurrected them as monsters, barely even recognizable as the people they once were.

"...How...dare you...?!"

Riselia's silvery hair lit up with an intense mana glow. She was furious at the Void Lord who had sullied the knights' souls. Fate had already stolen everything from her six years ago, and this was just another twist of the knife.

The Voids stood to bar the vehicle's path forward.

"Black Lightning, Flashing Through the Demonic Night, Shatter These Wandering Souls... Vuras Reiya!" Hanging onto Riselia's waist with one hand, Leonis chanted a sixth-order annihilation spell. Bolts of ebon electricity thundered forth, destroying the Voids in a single blow.

"Miss Riselia, I'm sorry, but these creatures are already..."

"...Yeah. I know," Riselia replied, holding back her sorrow. "Please put them to rest. It's the least we can do."

"Okay." Leonis nodded and began another spell.

Not being thorough in their destruction would mean their souls would continue wandering through these ruins. That was why Leonis used magic of fifth order or greater.

"Gather in My Hands, the True Fire That Consumes All—Al Gu Belzelga!"

The eighth-order fire spell burned the Voids away as soon as they manifested, destroying even the tears they emerged from. The sounds of battle filled the highway as Riselia urged the vehicle faster.

It wasn't until the Voids had all been slain that Leonis realized the Holy Sect hymn had died down.

What?

Filled with a grim sense of premonition, Leonis looked up at the Void Lord. Instead of a song, the thing was now reciting an incantation. Countless magic circles, a number large enough to obscure the sky, appeared over the Holy Woman.

That's...!

The next moment, a shower of burning meteors rained down from the many conjured arrays.

◆

Brrrrrrrrrrr, boom! Brrrrrrrrr, boom!

A shower of fire and brimstone barreled down from the heavens. Pillars of flame shot up in the Central Garden. It was like a vision of the end times.

"...Wh-what...? What's going on?!" Elfiné whispered in shock.

"That's an eleventh-order area destruction spell," Arle Kirlesio muttered. "The Smiting of the Heavenly Stars, Io Nemesis... Damn monster."

"...L-Lady Selia, kid, can you hear me?!" Regina tried to contact the other two members of the eighteenth platoon for what felt like the dozenth time, but there was still no response.

The Eye of the Witch orb Riselia and Leonis had with them may have been destroyed in the explosion. Elfiné turned their vehicle off the road and toward the bridge that led to the Central Garden.

The plumes of flame had died down, but ash and dirt choked the air.

"Elfiné. They're coming," Sakuya said suddenly, manifesting Raikirimaru in her hands.

"Huh?"

Crack....!

A massive fissure ran through the air in front of the four. At first, Elfiné thought the windshield had cracked, but she soon realized it was one of the fissures that heralded the arrival of Voids.

The next moment, the fracture erupted, and innumerable gray hands burst out of it.

"...?!"

Elfiné nearly hit the brakes but changed her mind at the last second. Stopping now would mean everyone would fall prey to the Voids.

"Hang on tight!"

Stomping down on the accelerator pedal, Elfiné pushed ahead. The vehicle rammed into the Voids, knocking them away as it ran over the bridge at full speed. Unfortunately, more cracks in space appeared up ahead.

"...This is just like what happens before a Stampede...!" Regina observed, manifesting Drag Striker in her hands and shooting down the Voids in their path.

"Elfiné, they're coming from above, too!" Sakuya shouted, cutting down Voids that had leaped from gaps above.

Curiously, even as chaos raged all around her, Arle Kirlesio kept her eyes fixed on the floating Void Lord. Her green ponytail danced in the wind.

"Sit down! It's dangerous!" Regina called out to her.

"Listen. I need you to do me a favor," Arle said, her gaze refusing to budge from the monster floating over the Central Garden.

◆

The highway was little more than chunks of stone now. The Third Assault Garden had been buffeted with meteors. The barren land was dotted with craters.

"Eleventh-order holy magic, the Smiting of the Heavenly Stars... That's some impressive power," Leonis said, standing in the center of the overwhelming destruction. He'd erected a Power Spot Barrier to protect Riselia and himself.

Looking around, he eyed the demolished two-wheeled vehicle. Though the Void Lord's spell had blown everything away, other Voids included, the attack hadn't been explicitly directed at Leonis. The Holy Woman hadn't even paid his presence any heed.

"Are you all right, Miss Selia?" asked Leonis.

"Ugh... Y-yeah..." Riselia moaned, sitting behind him and cradling her head. She was a bit dizzy from the shock of being knocked off the vehicle. Had Leonis chanted the incantation for his Power Spot Barrier spell any later, she wouldn't have gotten out of this unscathed, even with a Vampire Queen's vitality.

Leonis looked up at the sky. Floating above the clouds of dust it had kicked up, Tearis Resurrectia had begun to move again.

Is it trying to leave the Central Garden?

Leonis chanted a gravity control spell to fly up, then landed on a higher piece of the highway.

"You're not getting away," Leonis spat with a dauntless smile. He raised the Staff of Sealed Sins with both hands as he began chanting a grand feat of sorcery.

"Ashes to Ashes, Dust to Dust, Obey Thy Fated Ruin—Arzam!"

A magic circle formed at the tip of Leonis's rod, and from it burst a tenth-order spell that boasted destructive power of the highest level.

Booooooooooouooom!

A massive sphere of destruction expanded and then shot forward. It shook the earth as it traveled. The sheer power of this magic was enough to strike down a low-ranking god.

However, the Void Lord's massive shadow stood haughtily despite the flames licking at its form. Anti-Void weapons it had incorporated into itself had coated its body like armor, but now they melted away, revealing white flesh beneath that writhed like tentacles. The Void Lord then glowed faintly as its body began to regenerate.

Tearis Resurrectia's healing powers.

The monster shook off even a tenth-order destruction spell. It continued to float along in the air, chanting its holy hymn all the while.

The Archsage still seemed to have some of his intelligence left, but this one...

Arakael Degradios, while significantly decayed and corrupted, had retained a portion of his intellect and consciousness. The same could not be said of the Holy Woman.

Yes, I'm definitely overthinking this, Leonis decided, relieved. *I was foolish even to consider that a Void Lord could be Roselia's vessel. Her noble soul would never incarnate into such a mindless monster. But if that's the case, what did Nefakess mean by "goddess"?*

Either way, it was clear that Nefakess was involved in this Void Lord's awakening.

So be it. I will eventually drag him before me and have him speak. For now...

"Holy Woman of the Six Heroes, Tearis Resurrectia." Leonis gripped the hilt of the Staff of Sealed Sins. "You pitiful creature who has succumbed to the Voids. I shall visit eternal destruction upon you this day."

Leonis twisted the hilt of his staff, removing the dragon jewel inlaid at its tip. With this, he drew forth the Demon Sword sealed within the rod.

Thou Art the Sword to Save the World, Gifted by the Heavens.

Thou Art the Sword to Ruin the World, Made to Rebel Against the Heavens.

A Holy Sword, Sanctified by the Gods.

A Demon Sword, Blessed by the Goddess.

Tearis Resurrectia was a hero with the power to heal and revive. Perhaps Leonis could have defeated her with sorcery alone when he was the Undead King. However, now that he was in the body of a boy, destroying her with his spells would be difficult. Thus, Leonis drew the Demon Sword, a deity-slaying weapon given to him by Roselia, the Goddess of Rebellion.

Leonis could only release the seal on the weapon if his kingdom was in danger, and he'd fulfilled that condition. The blade of the Demon Sword blazed with malevolence.

As if reacting to the fearsome power of the Demon Sword, the Void Lord, who had thus far ignored Leonis, was now turning to face him.

So you finally deign to recognize me. I'm afraid it's too late now, however...

Leonis drew out the Demon Sword, keeping the dark light it unleashed contained.

Let Your Name, Submerged in Darkness, Ring Forth—

"The Demon Sword, Dáinsleif!"

"Perish, ye of the Six Heroes!" Leonis held up the Demon Sword with both hands

But just as he filled the sword with mana and prepared to swing down...

Kriiiiiiiiiiiiiiiiiiii! Dáinsleif let out a terrible screech.

The Demon Sword is resonating?! Leonis shook in confusion. This was a markedly different reaction from when he'd faced Arakael.

It can't be... No, there's no way that's true...!

That moment of doubt made Leonis lose control of the Demon Sword's power. In the same instant, the Void Lord's mana furnace lit up with a blinding flash.

Oh no.

A blade of pale light, bright enough to white out the area, ran through Leonis's body.

CHAPTER 9

THE DEMON SWORD'S PURPOSE

"...eo... Leo...!"

He could hear a voice desperately calling out to him.

"...Ugh... Aah..."

He opened his eyes, lying faceup, only to find Riselia peering down at him, her argent hair shining and tears glistening in her ice-blue eyes.

Aaah. You're so beautiful, my minion. Despite the dire situation, Leonis found his mind occupied by a rather odd thought.

The Dark Lord tried to move, an effort that only rewarded him with a horrible pain that shot through his side. He'd failed to evade the Void Lord's attack, which had sent him plummeting to the earth. Blood gushed out of the wound, pooling on the ground.

A human body is so painfully brittle and frail... So utterly incorrigible...

Gasping for air, Leonis mouthed half-formed curses. He could tell the strength was rapidly leaving his body. This was a sensation he'd long forgotten since gaining an undead body.

"Leo, are you all right?! Leo...!"

As Riselia's voice grew distant, Leonis turned his eyes to his right hand. Even with his consciousness fading, he didn't let go of

Dáinsleif. He couldn't, for it was the sword she had entrusted to him. It was his greatest memento of her. The Demon Sword's blade still pulsated with ebon light.

Dáinsleif, a sword created by the Goddess of Rebellion...reacted to the Void Lord.

What did that imply?

Has Roselia been reborn as the Void Lord?

Leonis had gone into magical stasis for a millennium to protect the human vessel that the Goddess of Rebellion was supposed to be reincarnated into one day.

I awakened in this world again to keep my promise to her.

He'd sworn to find her again, even in this strange world so detached from his own. However, if Roselia had truly been reborn as that terrible monster...

For... For what purpose did I...?

The Void Lord drew closer, little by little, and as it closed the distance, the Demon Sword began to react more powerfully.

"Miss...Selia... Run..." Leonis parted his lips as his mind grew murky from the blood loss. If nothing else, he wanted Riselia to survive. It was because of Leonis that she became his minion, after all. "Regroup with Regina and the others... And escape..."

"Leo!" Riselia shouted at him, almost scoldingly.

Kneeling down on the ground, she clutched Leonis's powerless form.

"What are you...? Ugh..."

A sweet pain rain through Leonis's neck. Riselia's small fangs bit into him.

"You already...drank my blood earlier...," Leonis whispered with a bitter, exhausted smile.

But then he realized... This was different. She wasn't draining him...

She's sharing...her blood with me...?

Leonis's heart thumped hard. He could tell that Riselia's blood was circulating through his body. His chest grew warm at the pure, gallant act of his minion. But...

It's...too late...

Leonis sank into the dark...

◆

"...Please?"

Elfiné turned around to look while pressing the pedal as hard as she could. Arle Kirlesio pointed at the Central Garden ahead of them.

"I need to get to the tallest tower. That one over there. Please, take me there."

Looking ahead at where Arle was pointing, Elfiné saw a skyscraper that was still mostly in one piece.

"And what are you going to do when you get there?" Regina asked as she shot down the Voids farther along the road.

"I will defeat that monster."

Elfiné and Regina exchanged concerned looks.

"Defeat it...? That's a Void Lord."

"I know. I came here to kill it," Arle declared, holding up her sword in front of Regina.

"So that sword is...," Sakuya muttered as she slashed a Void that had tried to climb onto the vehicle.

"Yes, it's a Holy Sword made to destroy that thing."

Sakuya nodded at Arle.

"Elfiné, I think you should do what she says."

"Sakuya..."

"We're heading to the Central Garden either way, and going up there might make it easier to find Selia and the kid."

"...I guess you're right."

"Understood. Arle, I'm putting my faith in your Holy Sword's power."

"...I won't let you down." Arle nodded firmly with her weapon at the ready.

"The only problem is whether we can get there...," Regina observed. Voids were appearing nonstop, just like during a Stampede.

Crack... Crack... Crack...!

Suddenly, a massive fissure appeared in front of the group's vehicle.

"...What?!"

It was a colossal fracture that dwarfed all the ones that had come before it. A statue of a giant with glowing wings erupted from within that crack.

"...This is bad. That angel is—!" Arle shouted.

"Goooooooooooooohhhhhhhhhhh...!" the giant howled, swinging its rocklike arms down on the vehicle.

Elfiné turned the steering wheel hard to one side, but it wasn't enough to dodge in time. The Void's limbs were simply too massive.

"...?!"

It was going to crush them. Elfiné squeezed her eyes shut. But then...

Whiiish!

A black whip coiled around the enormous arm and hurled the Void away in what seemed like a casual gesture.

Booooooooooooooom!

The huge Void went flying off the bridge and into the sea below, creating a gigantic splash of water.

"Wh-what was that?!" Regina exclaimed.

"...I don't know. But...," Elfiné replied. This was their chance to break through. Using the Eye of the Witch's powers to cancel the vehicle's speed limiter, Elfiné floored the acceleration pedal.

As the vehicle sped off, a small girl remained behind, perched on one of the bridge's supporting poles. She turned her wrist lightly, retracting the length of her shadow whip to her hand. Her dusk-colored eyes saw the vehicle off and then turned to peer into the water below.

The surface of the sea swelled, and the angel-class Void rose from its depths.

"You look like a fun enough toy to play around with," the girl mused, running her fingers over her lips with a faint smile. "As a maid loyal to her master, I shall be your opponent."

The Realm of Shadows' umbral maid pinched up the hems of her skirt politely in a curtsy.

♦

"...Leonis... Leonis, listen..."

He could hear a voice in the darkness. It was that of a girl. She sounded a bit younger than she should have been. Her slender fingers gently caressed his hair.

"I need you to promise me. In the distant future, if I change and become something else..." She smiled sadly. "I want you to kill me with that Demon Sword."

"...Wh-what are you saying?! I could never do that!" the boy exclaimed, shaking off her hand.

"Even if I ask you to?"

"Of course! I... I could never..."

The boy shook his head. Tears welled up in the corners of his eyes. The girl embraced him gently.

"Understood. I'm sorry. Forget I said that. But..." She drew close to whisper in the boy's ears. "But *if that day comes...* I want you to remember. My wish, and your purpose. And then... *Please find the real me.* I'm sure the Demon Sword I gave you will guide you to your fate."

◆

That...was no dream. It was my memory...

Leonis felt his heart thrum hard as he was yanked back to the waking world. He'd recalled something she'd said to him over one thousand years ago. It was a promise that Leonis had forgotten.

Why did that memory...?

Leonis's eyes opened.

"...eo... Leo...?!"

"Miss...Selia..."

Riselia's arms were wrapped around Leonis's head. Just like when he first awakened in Necrozoa's mausoleum. He could still feel faint, sweet pangs of pain on his neck, and he could sense mana running through his body. Riselia had shared it with him along with her blood.

I see. Maybe these memories...

Riselia had consumed Leonis's blood and mana many times. Remnants of those recollections may have mixed in with the blood she took from him. And with it returned to him, the memory had awakened. Was such a thing even possible?

Leonis himself wasn't entirely certain, but it was the only explanation he could come up with. A promise he'd made with the goddess Roselia in the far past—an oath he'd forgotten.

No... She had sealed the memory away.

Riselia had locked it away so that when the time came, Leonis would remember his purpose. If her reincarnation failed, and she ceased being herself, he would put her down with the very weapon she had gifted to him.

That was the mission she entrusted me with...

Leonis gripped Dáinsleif. Had the Goddess of Rebellion foreseen that the Voids would twist her noble soul?

But if this is my purpose, to what end did I...?

"Leo..." Riselia gently caressed Leonis's back as he shook.

"I...made a promise," the Dark Lord breathed.

"Yeah." Riselia nodded. "What kind of promise?"

"That I would find her, no matter what. And..."

On that day, Leonis had sworn that, even if it was far into the future, he would find her no matter what. He would locate the *real her.*

...?! Something struck Leonis like a bolt from above. *The real... her...?* The boy's eyes went wide.

She'd definitely said, "I want you to find the real me."

Leonis looked at Dáinsleif's blade as it pulsed in chorus with the Void Lord. Roselia's voice, as he remembered it, surfaced in his mind:

"I'm sure the Demon Sword I gave you will guide you to your fate."

What could that have meant?

Roselia gave me this weapon to kill her.

If that Void Lord was the true vessel for her soul...*he never would have been able to draw it against her.* That much was clear. She was the Demon Sword's true master, after all.

I see. So that is what this is all about...

Dáinsleif was beckoning Leonis to strike down this fallen, false god—guiding him to seek out Roselia Ishtaris's real soul.

The actual task she gave me was...

Leonis grabbed onto Riselia's arm with one hand and pulled himself to his feet wordlessly.

"Leo...?"

"I'm fine now, Miss Selia—"

Leonis shook his head and faced the approaching Void Lord, the False God of Nothingness that housed the Goddess of Rebellion's soul.

"*Ooooh... Oooh... Oooh, ooooooooooh...!*" The Holy Woman's song summoned a small army of humanoid Voids. Cracks ran through the air. Dozens of gray arms crept from them and grasped at Leonis and Riselia.

"While I'm using the Demon Sword, I'll be essentially defenseless. Can you keep me safe?"

"...Yeah. Leave it to me, Leo." Riselia nodded with a smile. Even when Voids surrounded them, her eyes didn't betray a hint of fear.

Such is my worthy minion. A dauntless smile played over Leonis's lips.

Confidence aside, Riselia would have trouble holding back this many Voids on her own. Leonis held the Demon Sword overhead.

"Loyal armies of the Realm of Death, gather at my beck and call!" He raised his voice in a clear, resounding command. The shadow at his feet expanded, painting the ground around him black.

Rattle... Rattle, rattle, rattle... Rattle, rattle, rattle...

An army of hundreds upon thousands crawled out. This was one of Leonis's eighth-order anti-army spells—Form Undead Army. Unfortunately, it could only create low-ranking skeletons that were no match for the Voids.

These soldiers are but bone puppets that operate on my mana. However...

If brave warriors' souls could possess those empty vessels, it would make for a different story. And as the Undead King,

Leonis could feel the Crystalia Knights' spirits still trapped in this ruined city.

These brave warriors' souls still longed to fight alongside Riselia Crystalia.

Then, as a Dark Lord, I shall grant your wish! Leonis relinquished control over the undead horde. Immediately, the eye sockets of the soldiers lit up with a crimson glow. They began rattling their teeth in distorted laughter, an expression of their boundless joy at the chance to wield swords in battle again.

"Leo, what is this...?" Riselia took in the sight of the chattering skeletons with a confused expression on her face. An ordinary girl would've undoubtedly passed out at such a scene.

"The souls of the Crystalia Knights occupy these skeletons. Miss Selia, lead them to battle."

"Huh? Me?!"

"Please. I need you to hold back the Void hordes for as long as you can."

"...Understood!" Riselia nodded, her look of surprise becoming one of determination.

Her silvery hair lit up, and her ice-blue eyes turned crimson. Mana enveloped her body, coiling around her to form a beautiful red dress. She stood dignified, the Bloody Sword in hand, the very image of a Vampire Queen. With her Holy Sword held high, she commanded, "Brave Knights of House Crystalia! Follow me!"

The army of skeleton soldiers clicked their teeth in response.

◆

As the battle between undead and Voids began in earnest, a red flower bloomed upon the battlefield.

"Aaaaaaaaaaaaaah!"

Riselia slashed her way through, the hem of the True Ancestor's Dress fluttering as she strode forward. The Bloody Sword gave off an ominous glow, leaving red trails through the air. The blood running across its edge turned to blades that went flying in all directions.

The humanoid Voids were the defiled souls of those who had fought for the Third Assault Garden in the past. But this truth did little to make Riselia falter. Her Holy Sword would destroy their souls, freeing them. That is what drove Riselia forward.

She continued to slash through the Voids, and her skeleton followed the crimson glow of her weapon. It felt as if all the power in her body had been unlocked. Strength seemed to pour from her. The dress Leonis had given her devoured her mana rapidly, but it forcibly drew out her Vampire Queen power in exchange.

It's consuming more mana than I thought.

If this skirmish was to last much longer, it would surely deplete Riselia. As she cut through one Void after the next, she snuck a glance in Leonis's direction. He stood above the rubble, his Demon Sword pointing up at the heavens. Over his head, a small black moon was beginning to take shape.

That moon... Riselia furrowed her brow suspiciously. Every time a skeleton fell in battle, a stream of light flitted out of its remains and was swallowed up by that obsidian sphere. Each one that fed the moon made it grow larger.

Are those the Crystalia Knights' souls...?! Just as Riselia came to that shocking realization...

"Graaaaaaaaaaaah!"

A Void lunged at her, brandishing its sharp claws.

"...!"

"Milady!"

A spiky iron ball connected to a chain smashed into the Void's

head. A hulking skeleton wearing heavy armor had hurled the weapon right in the nick of time.

"You mustn't be careless, princess!" chided Dorug, the grappler.

"Indeed! The power of the Vampire Queen is vast, but you mustn't grow overconfident."

"We shall fight alongside you!"

The archmage Nefisgal and the swordsman Amilas stood at Riselia's side, their weapons in hand.

"Thank you! You saved me there..."

Without a moment to lose, Riselia rejoined the fight, her crimson dress dancing in the wind. Her Bloody Sword raged with mana, sweeping through Voids.

Six years ago, I couldn't protect anything.

Riselia had only been able to cower and pray for salvation. Now, she had the power to protect herself and others. The Holy Sword the planet had given to her, and the might of the Vampire Queen...

The silver-haired girl's overflowing mana left trails of red as it cut through the air. The Voids gathered around her, as if drawn to that glow.

"...Aaaaaaaaaaah!" Riselia moved to force her way out of this encirclement. But just then...

Boom, boom, boom!

Flashes of light burst forth like shooting stars, piercing through the Voids' heads with pinpoint accuracy.

"...?!" Riselia turned around with a start, only to find...

◆

Four figures stood on the rooftop of a ruined skyscraper. Regina had her Drag Striker readied and was sniping the Voids from afar with deadly aim. She didn't use the more powerful Drag Blast for fear of hitting Riselia.

"I can't really see anything in that huge mess. What are all those skeletons?!" Regina exclaimed.

"That's probably the power of Leo's Holy Sword...," Elfiné answered while holding a hand up to her temple.

Three Eye of the Witch orbs floated around her. A stream of luminous numbers ran across them.

Even a skilled sharpshooter like Regina couldn't accurately hit targets at such a great distance using only the naked eye. Elfiné's Holy Sword calculated the trajectory of Regina's shots to support her.

"How's it going on your end?"

"Just a little longer...," Arle Kirlesio replied.

With one of the Arc Seven—the Demon Smiting Sword, Crozax—held in her hands, she filled the blade with mana.

"They're climbing up, Elfiné," Sakuya observed, swinging Raikirimaru to cut down a force of Voids that tried to scale the walls.

Despite her efforts, there were too many of them. Regina moved from supporting Riselia to assisting Sakuya in staving off the Void onslaught. Raikirimaru's blade crackled with electricity as it flashed through the air, decapitating the monsters in fast succession.

With horrifying howls and the sound of clashing metal echoing around her, Arle closed her eyes. Crozax was a hero's weapon, entrusted to her to slay the goddess. The fierce sheen of the blade whited out the air around the half-elf.

"...Is that really a Holy Sword?!" Regina exclaimed, shielding her eyes.

"Roselia Ishtaris, the Goddess of Rebellion! I will strike you down!"

Unleashing all the mana in her body, Arle loosed Crozax's power!

♦

Back on the battlefield, as skeletons clashed with distorted monsters, Leonis faced the Void Lord floating above him. The Holy Woman, Tearis Resurrectia, now contained Roselia's soul.

However, that spirit both was and wasn't the Goddess of Rebellion. With his Demon Sword held aloft, Leonis looked up to the sky. A black moon glinted ominously above. It was a seventh-order spell of the Realm of Death—Suray Gira, the Blue Moon of the Dead. The ritual magic gathered wandering souls and converted them to mana.

The obsidian moon sucked up the Crystalia Knights' souls and swelled up to three times its size.

"Dead Ones, Let Your Mana Become My Own, as You Are Set Free From the Shackles That Bind Your Souls." At Leonis's command, the moon dispersed into particles of mana that gathered in the Demon Sword's blade.

Thou Art the Sword to Save the World, Gifted by the Heavens.
Thou Art the Sword to Ruin the World, Made to Rebel Against the Heavens.

A Holy Sword, Sanctified by the Gods.
A Demon Sword, Blessed by the Goddess.

Dáinsleif let out a dark glow, its blade swirling with massive amounts of mana. But at the same time...
"*Gooooooooooooooooohhhhhhhhhhhhh!*"

Many magic circles formed above the Void Lord. It was the same spell that had reduced the Central Garden to burning scrap in mere moments, the Smiting of the Heavenly Stars.

Again?! Now?!

Because he'd had to concentrate on controlling the Demon Sword's power, Leonis was utterly defenseless. He couldn't guard himself or chant a protective spell like last time.

Which one of us will finish first...?!

Suddenly, a flash of light fired from afar cleaved into the Void Lord's mana furnace.

What?! Leonis's eyes widened in shock.

A torrent of intense light blew away the spell that was on the verge of being completed, destroying the magic circles that had formed in the sky.

That attack just now... Was that Regina's Drag Blast? Or is this Shary's doing?

Either way, this was Leonis's chance. He focused back on Dáinsleif. The Void Lord let out a rumbling howl. The attack it had suffered was evidently quite substantial, though still not enough to slay the Holy Woman.

"Perish, Tearis Resurrectia of the Six Heroes, vessel to a false god...!"

Leonis swung Dáinsleif down, putting all the mana he had into the attack.

Whoooosh!

The overflowing, raging black light consumed the mana furnace, shattering it to pieces...and with this, the gigantic Void Lord began to crumble, collapsing in on itself like an old castle.

14:00 Imperial Standard Time.

Excalibur Academy's tactical fighter, the Lindwyrm Mk.III, departed after confirmation that the Third Assault Garden had ceased moving. Upon returning to the academy, Riselia and the rest of the eighteenth platoon would likely have to give a detailed report.

With the Void Lord's destruction, the possibility of another Stampede had been averted, and the wandering souls of the Crystalia Knights were free. Leonis felt a bit reluctant to give up on such strong spirits, but forcing warriors who'd fought for their homeland to remain under his command did not sit well with him.

Currently, Leonis occupied the tactical fighter's back seat, resting his head on Riselia's lap. Naturally, this was not something he'd requested. Using Dáinsleif had wholly exhausted his mana reserves, leaving him so drained he wouldn't be able to stand unassisted for some time.

Th-this is...entirely against my will...! Leonis made excuses for himself while Riselia loomed above, leafing through a book.

"What are you reading, Lady Selia?" Regina inquired.

"Something I found in Father's study. I thought I would take it with me as a memento."

"Hmm." Regina peeked at a few of the pages. "I don't recognize this language."

"Me neither. It doesn't look like spirit text..."

As Leonis listened in on their exchange, a thought crossed his mind. *Come to think of it, we never found Riselia's father among the wandering souls.*

Leonis had used his authority as the Undead King to examine the souls of the wandering ghosts, but none of them seemed to be Riselia's father.

Perhaps he was already turned into a Void? Or else...

It was then that Regina plopped a hand down on Leonis's head and said, "I'm sure you're tired, Miss Selia. How about you let me take over as the kid's lap pillow?"

"N-no! Leo's sleeping so soundly."

"You're being unfair, Lady Selia. You shouldn't hog him like that."

"...I am not hogging him, and it's not unfair!" Riselia exclaimed and cradled Leonis's head tightly.

Feeling the softness of her breasts through her clothes made Leonis's heart skip a beat.

"My apologies, you two, but could you be a little quieter?" Sakuya requested, raising a finger to her lips. "You might wake her up."

She was in the other row of seats. A half-elf girl in shorts was sleeping on her lap.

The Hero of the Sanctuary, Arle Kirlesio. Leonis gazed at the girl as she slumbered. Her dainty arms were wrapped around her weapon. Based on Shary's report, she'd been injured in the Third Assault Garden while fighting the Voids, and Regina's group had rescued her.

Leonis knew her. She was an apprentice to Shardark, the Swordmaster of the Six Heroes. He had taught Leonis back when he was still a human, which meant Arle was technically his sibling apprentice.

It was her attack that damaged the Void Lord.

Fortunately, Arle's strike had momentarily blinded Regina and the others, keeping them from seeing that Leonis had delivered the final blow. Thus, Regina, Elfiné, and Sakuya had the impression Arle was the one who'd felled the Void Lord. Leonis didn't mind. Their remaining unaware of his real power suited his needs well enough.

However, this elf girl had somehow appeared in this age much like Leonis had. Between her, the Six Heroes, and that man who had attacked in the Crystalia Estate, this didn't feel like a coincidence.

What are those dead fools planning? Leonis pondered, his head buried in Riselia's chest.

Nefakess Reizaad knew Roselia would incarnate into the Holy Woman.

A member of the Six Heroes became both a Void and Roselia's vessel. It was clear Nefakess was involved in this. His aims, however, remained unknown.

If he tried to use Roselia's soul in some way...

Leonis promised to visit vengeance upon Nefakess for his transgressions. Dark flames of anger burned silently in Leonis's heart.

"L-Leo, hey..."

Leo felt the thighs he was resting on fidget. Silvery locks brushed against his cheek as Riselia brought her lips to his ear. Apparently, she'd noticed he was awake.

"...Can I suck some blood, just a bit?" she asked, sticking out her adorable tongue and then gently nibbling on his earlobe.

"N-not here! Miss Regina and Miss Sakuya are right there!" Leonis replied, doing his best to keep his voice low so the others wouldn't notice.

"Yeah, so I'll be quiet about it..."

"No, they'll definitely notice us!"

"So I can't?"

"...No, you can't!"

"...L-Leo... I... I can't help it..."

Wh-what is this minion doing all of a sudden?!

Leonis stirred on Riselia's lap as he looked up at her face. Her pale cheeks were flushed, and her eyes glistened with desire. Her lips parted, and hot breaths escaped them. There was a feverish warmth to her fingertips.

That's when Leonis realized that it was because Riselia had shared her blood with him. It had left her with this crippling thirst.

"F-fine. I'll let you drink all you want when we get back to the dorm."

"...Can't you let me do it now?" Riselia pleaded.

"J-just be a patient for a while longer."

"...A-all right."

Riselia swallowed audibly, nibbling on Leonis's earlobe reproachfully from where Regina and the rest couldn't see her.

I guess I can allow this much. Leonis surrendered himself to Riselia's playful bites. He had regained that memory thanks to her, so conceding this much of a reward was acceptable.

As Leonis felt Riselia nibble on his ear, he thought on the meaning behind that promise.

"I want you to find the real me," she'd said.

It was Roselia's soul that possessed the Holy Woman. That much is for sure.

In which case, what had she meant by the real her? Was Roselia's soul split when she was reincarnated? If so, had it been of her own will?

The vessel for the Goddess of Rebellion's spirit was out there somewhere in this world. And seeking it out was Leonis Magnus's mission as a Dark Lord.

Roselia, I will find you. I swear it.

As sleep overtook him, Leonis clenched his fists in silent resolve.

↺AFTERWORD

Thank you for your patience, kind readers! My name is Yu Shimizu. This is Volume 3 of *The Demon Sword Master of Excalibur Academy*, a school sword fantasy starring the now-ten-year-old Dark Lord Leonis and the older girls who help him! This time, the stage was Riselia's birthplace, the Third Assault Garden. It was invaded and overrun by Voids six years ago. Leonis and the girls were dispatched to investigate the ruined city, and they wound up finding all sorts of mysterious things!

This time, the enemy finally starts to reveal itself, but there's still quite a bit of foreshadowing peppered throughout the story. I was constantly checking my notes all throughout writing this volume. It was a little challenging, but I think it made for a really packed narrative.

Much to my pleasant surprise, this series continues to sell at a breakneck pace, and we've reached a total of over one hundred thousand copies sold!

Volume 4 will add the slightly tsundere elf girl Arle, introduced in this book, to the main cast. Things only get more exciting from here, so I hope you'll look forward to it! Shary, Fluffymaru the

Black (aka Blackas), Leonis's third sealed minion, and even other Dark Lords are set to appear. Expect the plot to feature more elements from Leonis's past!

In addition, *The Demon Sword Master of Excalibur Academy* now has a serialized manga adaptation in *Monthly Shounen Ace* magazine, drawn by Asuka Keigen! Leonis and Riselia are quite expressive, and the combat scenes are all exciting! Do check it out.

A special promotional video and mini voice drama are also being produced for the series. The super-popular voice actress Nao Toyoma is playing both Riselia and Leonis! Can you believe it? Personally, I'm really looking forward to it. Nao Toyoma performs Riselia's voice exactly as I imagined it!

Lastly, some thanks.

To Asagi Tosaka, for providing the gorgeous cover art and insert illustrations for this volume despite the tight schedule, thank you so much! I have the pinup you drew of Riselia up on my wall, and she's so beautiful that I can spend minutes just looking at her.

To the editors, designers, and proofreaders, my sincerest gratitude for all your help with this volume. It's because of you that we were able to release this book to the world!

However, my most heartfelt thanks are for you all, the readers who picked up this book! I'll do my best to see this become an even more spectacular series. I hope you'll continue to support my works. Your thoughts on the series are a great source of encouragement for me, so do send them my way!

The next volume will take us back to Excalibur Academy. I hope you're looking forward to it.

—Yu Shimizu, December 2019